SCRIP-CRAZY

TOO

By

Martin Kay

Cork, Ireland

INTRODUCTION

I wish to make it completely clear that I am an enthusiastic supporter of the availability of stroke treatment in every hospital. I am even more grateful for, and appreciative of, the care provided for stroke victims in Cork University Hospital (CUH) and St Finbarre's, Ireland. The word 'victim' is an ugly word but that's what happens to you with stroke. The experience can be like walking into a railway engine – total wipe out. They tell me that for some their stroke is much milder. Those are the lucky ones. I was not but, oddly enough, improved my chances of survival because I realised myself what was happening to me. I realised myself – and began shouting for help. And the medics and clinicians within earshot provided that help, just in time.

If you read this book, however, you will realise that things began to go wrong for me before I realised what was actually happening. I could have called for help much earlier but I didn't. I urge you, all of you, to call for help if ever you feel that something isn't right. The slightest thing. Don't wait. Call for help as quickly and as loudly as you can. And get someone to take you to hospital if an ambulance isn't available.

Don't be embarrassed. It is your life we are talking about.

So, what is this book about? Well, it goes beyond that calamity of the stroke. I realised that I was venturing into a strange world – a world that had been written about by someone in the middle of the 20th century. If he can write about it, I thought, then I can too.

This book is about the effect of drugs. Prescription drugs. We cannot do without prescription drugs but that does not mean that we cannot write about them. This is a tale of recent events and moderately unusual life experience woven through a compendium of things my damaged mind wants to say. There was not much conspicuously out of the ordinary about the undamaged Me to make my thoughts exceptional – at least I don't think there was. But what follows here has been written under the influence of a sustained pharmaceutical assault upon my mind and nervous system, hence the name Scrip-Crazy. One of the drugs I have taken for the last 21 months, at the rate of 300mg x 3 doses x 3 times daily, would worry me greatly were it not for the standing of the Consultants who first prescribed it and still monitor my progress. But that amount of daily Neurontin

(Gabapentin), multiplied by 20 months, must be changing something.

In a way, I am like the late Aldous Huxley who was concerned about the dangers of scientific progress and described the effects of a particular drug upon the mind and imagination. But in several ways, I am not.

Huxley *experimented* – most famously, in a 1956 essay entitled 'Heaven and Hell' – with the drug Mescaline. I suffered a severe stroke in February 2019 and take my drugs *under medical prescription*: none of them is or contains Mescaline. Furthermore, I had never knowingly taken, or experimented with, any drugs beyond alcohol and tobacco before the year 2013 when my health went into decline. From then until the date of my stroke, February 2019, I was prescribed what to my mind was an appalling rate of antibiotics (an alternating cocktail of mostly, but not exclusively, Augmentin, Clarithromycin, Doxycycline Teva, Amycin, Betnesol and similar ear drops) for chronic sinusitis, pneumonia, serious ear infections and related conditions. Before then, I was robust and sturdily healthy. Since February 2019, I have spent an aggregate 12 months in hospital and 12 months in 'isolation' at home. Throughout the years, all the years, my diet has been mostly sensible and restrained. I stopped smoking in 1989 and have not consumed alcohol since the date of my stroke. My consumption of alcohol before then was not excessive. I enjoyed two or three glasses of red wine, French or Italian, and the occasional pint of Murphy's stout.

I need in further amplification to say that I have also ingested under prescription since 2012-13 a frightening quantity of the steroid Deltacortril. When I say 'frightening', the quantity must now in January 2021 be easily, easily, approaching 6,000 x 5mg tablets.

Apparently they are meant to have no lasting effect but I reject that. Steroids are also present in my other prescribed daily medicines in various quantities. I keep them all in a box which I have labelled 'Puffs and Squirts'. And that reveals my contempt for 'being ill' and all that it entails. None of it will get me down.

On re-reading the preceding paragraph, I realise, too, that I self-prescribed an excessive, and probably unwise, amount of pseudoephedrine in the over-the-counter tablet form of Sudafed between 2013 and 2018. This was for my sinus condition. That may be one reason why my 'water-works' are not functioning properly – a warning that is clearly stated in the manufacturer's leaflet. *Mea culpa*. Read the leaflet extra carefully if ever you see a product with an 'eff' sound in it. Don't make taking it to excess an instance of *tua culpa*.

Notwithstanding, I wish to state clearly and unequivocally that I feel I have been blessed with outstanding medical, clinical and pharmaceutical care throughout the last eight years. I am equally sure that the Me who taps one-fingered now is not the Me who came to grief in mid-February of 2019 and certainly not the Me who started this downward cycle in 2012/13. I list the remainder of the drugs I am ingesting daily towards the end of this tale.

Apart from Paracetamol and Aspirin, I recognise none of their names. I am determined that none of them will get me down but, in a way, it is not so much the daily intake of these pills that worries me but a small dosage of 'mood-lifters' I was advised to take while in hospital over a year ago. I took them on three occasions – not more than three doses on each occasion, and probably fewer; and possibly the same drug repeated once but not, I am fairly certain, twice. Those are the ones that really worry me.

He had woken up after three months in a coma. On a bed but in a coma. Looking back it was mostly a social coma. It had never occurred to him that there might be more than one. Coma, that is. Not just being medically switched off, but three months of being institutionalised with the brain numbed off, too. A *double* coma. Institutionalised without even a 'point him at the door' or 'get out of jail free' card, which at least would have given him some chance of realising where the way out lay and how to use it. Three months of feeling imprisoned. Out of it. Not conscious. Half-conscious, if not constantly asleep then longing to be so and yet still longing to be well away and back to normal. Whatever normal is. Was.

There was not even a 'teach-yourself' vocabulary book to break the monotony whenever he was awake. Not even anything.

Just the window with its world beyond. His tireless, beautiful wife brought him anything inside the window. Anything but not everything, although they thought she did. They took his concept of everything away, you see, and she could not replace it. No, you don't see. He could tell.

"Don't you understand," he asked, clutching at one fading recollection, "I am a writer. I routinely start work at four o'clock in the morning."

"Don't *you* understand," they replied, dealing solely with the present. "You are in hospital now. At four o'clock in the morning, you sleep." There was venom in the latter instruction. Uncharacteristic venom. And shorter sentences. He obeyed. Well, at least he closed his eyes and kept them shut. It occurred to him that nurses could probably see in the dark which was more than he could.

'Lunchtime' was the next thing they said. But not to him, to her and for a different reason. Let's just see if he can make it to lunchtime. Yes, he is ... very ill. Tea-time. Take it a bit at a time ... Let's just see ... We'll see you tomorrow. Yes, we'll be here. No, we think you have brought him everything. Keep going, *keep going*. But she didn't go. She just sat there beside his bed. They went while the pair of them stayed behind. Silent while the night staff somehow materialised in their place. Even the tap dripped louder than their hopes.

Eventually, they changed their tune and began to speak to him. He deduced, therefore, that his crisis had passed. *Re*-hab, they announced. You will *love* it there. They enthused about *Re*-hab. Everyone did. A bed is coming up. Next week some time. No, tomorrow. It looks like tomorrow. *Re-hab.*You'll see!

They couldn't get him out of the ward fast enough, this trouble-maker who routinely wanted his own routines. Out of the ward, they went. Down the corridor. Oh! Forgotten something. Turn on the spot, back up the corridor. Got it? Got it, he replied. Out of the ward down the corridor left at the end turn by the lifts, Level 1? he asked. Yup, says the porter.

Yup, he replied, pressing level 1 for him, and then they waited.

Sudden activity. A lift is coming. Oh, oh. A porter 'driving' a bed with an unspeakably ill-looking patient inside just pushed past them and squeezed into the available space. The bed had right of way over the wheelchair. The bed disappeared inside the lift and, outside, they started to wait again. A bit fell off the chair. The left foot plate. It did that all the time. They located, re-positioned and re-secured the foot plate. And then they started watching again. They watched an inbound patient lying on a bed in the corridor, waiting for a space inside …

"Give him mine," he had offered uselessly on several occasions. "I really don't mind being in the corridor". (He was thinking piously at the time of John Stuart Mills' thoughts on 'liberty' – oh God, came a despairing voice from somewhere underneath him. Underneath?
The wheelchair? His thoughts moved on.)

And then once, he actually went and stood in the corridor in order to make his protest.
'Stood' is not the best word for it – he lurched his way out there, dragged himself and then sagged against, and slipped down, a

convenient wall until ordered to return inside. Ordered. And again, he obeyed. Marched inside, but this time with his eyes open and by the scruff of his pyjama collar.

… and when they felt embarrassed at being caught staring at the inbound patient, they watched the lifts busy themselves up and down between Levels G and 1 and the floors between 1 and the wheelchair, but never as far as that. It seemed as if they couldn't make contact in any direction except with the person on the bed who had long since disappeared.

Eventually, one lift breaks through and rises up in their direction. Yes, it's stopping.

Someone gets out, a woman is staying in and they squeeze in beside her.

Hello, he mumbled. She sniffs and tightens her folded arms under her buttoned bosom.

He turned his head away, realising that he had also left his favourite pen behind in the ward.

Nay, I am no' goin' back. Ah cannae be borthered, he muttered in mock-Glaswegian.

Evidently, he had spoken out loud for it seems to have rung some inner bell within the tightened corset which relaxed and produced a piece of chewing gum (unused, he was relieved to see) which she held in his direction. It seems she came from Lesmahagow, the unlovely name of a town near Glasgow. "Ah, Wogahamsel!" he exclaimed, knowing the old joke. "Aye," she said. And, gallantly and with relief, they waved her first off the lift when they finally reached Level 1.

All the world and its wheelchairs seem to be waiting on Level 1, looking begrudgingly at them as the porter shoved his wheelchair out on to the landing. The porter muttered something to a colleague waiting to get in and go up but he and his wheelchair didn't understand what he was saying. They had suddenly, without warning come from the Moors of Lanarkshire, just south-east of Glasgow, to the lovely coastline of Cork in Ireland. The wheelchair came from Cork city. Its occupant had lived in both and, until his stroke and since, he still lived in the latter. He was proficient in both Highland and Lowland Scots as well as Ulster Irish but understandably, in the south-west Irish province of Munster, could rarely find a harmonious or intelligible connection from which to learn. Something said without warning could pass him by and even deny him the opportunity of making an observation to indicate that he might have understood. An observation to show that his limbs may look crippled but he was certain he was not mentally deficient. Not completely. The wheelchair might be crook but he wasn't. Good grief, he glared back at an insolent stare from some passer-by, there *is* a brain in here. He had written six books. He also had a PhD but it was in something he couldn't remember.

That's right, you can't remember, squeaked the wheelchair in reproof, what you spent eight years studying – I can remember how my left foot plate works but you can only remember the gown and the hat. The bunnet, its occupant corrected the wheelchair back into wersh-Scotch. Some of it wuz red. Aye, the coat I had on. Ut wuz red too, Jummy, ut wuz red too. Oh God, take me to Re-hab.

Please, please, take us to Re-hab, agreed the wheelchair.

Re-hab, the wheelchair corrected both itself and its occupant – and then petulantly it continued, and my name isn't Jummy. Curiously, he was unsurprised to discover that his wheelchair thought and talked. Why shouldn't anything express an opinion on life in this bizarre half-drugged world?

They sat for a while in the main entrance to the hospital, watching the froth and mingle of sick people and well, of patients and families, of clinicians and medics, and so on and endlessly on. They saw the Bishop on his way to offer crosses and blessings in A&E and one of their two illustrious members of the Dáil[1] seeking crosses and coffee in the cafeteria. I can tell you, he confided in the wheelchair, it's bloody

---

[1] The lower house of the Irish State's bicameral parliamentary system. At the time of writing, the author's constituency boasted the deputy Prime Minister and the Leader of the Opposition among its four elected representatives.

unnerving suddenly seeing the Bish materialise beside your pillow; a politician I could handle but the other fellow … well, I thought I was on the way out and that he had come to collect me.

In the meantime, work went on for everyone except the porter, the wheelchair and him, sat there in the spectacular round entrance lobby to Cork's University Hospital. It brought a whole new meaning, they agreed, to 'Bless me.'

He had been taken into just about every entrance to that hospital over recent years, even once into maternity but that was the result of a misunderstanding. Nothing to do with me, interjected the wheelchair pointedly while, briefly embarrassed, the porter looked the other way. His main route in was through A&E and he had come to the conclusion that he now deserved a medal for, at least, good attendance: 'Patient No. 999130 has performed consistently and satisfactorily. But with better transport .....' The left foot plate fell noisily off. Off noisily. Certainly, the atmosphere had changed for the worse.

He was now regularly recognised which was quite nice but his best 'entrance' in a stage sense was three months before they decided he was ready for *Re*-hab. It had happened in a residential road off the College Road in Cork and the wheelchair had nothing to do with it.

Nothing at all.

"Look!" she said, pointing sideways across me into a low, dazzling shaft of winter sunlight.

"Look what they are doing to that house."

I looked. Damn. *Damn!* "Everything's turning. I can't see straight," I shouted, lurching violently from the driver's seat across into her lap.

"Stop the jeep!" she screamed and I managed to grind it to a halt against the side of the pavement. Thank God there were no cars. From the noise, the wheels had been damaged and I suppose the pavement was, too. But we were alive and, more importantly, so were the people who lived there.

I somehow managed to make the spinning stop. But it happened again, twenty yards further on. Thank God there was no-one watching our progress.

Stubbornly, I insisted on driving home but it happened a third time, just round the corner on College Road itself. Thank God again that I didn't hit anyone and managed to pull round into the Brookfield entrance to the

University where I stopped. She leaped out, frantically seeking help and guidance. I heard her describing it all to someone I could not identify, finishing sadly: "I don't know what to do."

I couldn't help her – not least because I was unaware of what the Irish Heart Foundation had said about my condition –

– *condition?* I haven't got a condition, I thought. *I* have, said something with wheels on faintly in the background.

I just got dizzy, I continued. I haven't got any condition. Just hearing things, I thought.

In fact I was draped over the steering wheel showing no visible signs of life (and clearly did have some sort of condition). The front doors of the jeep were wide open and I was motionless, uncertain whether an attempt to get out would cause me to vomit violently or my bowels to evacuate spontaneously. A new voice close to my side asked if I was alright. Calming, courteous and re-assuring: "I'm a medical student," he added and then apologetically, "third year".

I spoke for the first time but not to laugh although, by this time, I felt like it. "Thank you for stopping. No, I can't get out and I don't feel any signs of something worse, so don't call an ambulance … I have stopped the vertigo and I think I will be able to get out soon. But stand back in case I throw up … I know the feeling, it will come out in a jet." Disgusting, I thought, recalling the filthy stream my gall bladder had occasionally produced. Better to warn them.

Don't get carried away, I continued, thinking aloud to myself . This has gone far enough and evidently there is something very wrong. *Ask for help, idiot.* But, idiot, I didn't,

I just kept gazing at the little of the world outside that I could see through the cracks in my fingers. I found security in doing nothing.

By the sound of their voices, my wife and the medical student had withdrawn from the range of my gall bladder. Soon they were joined by a new voice wearing a yellow surcoat.

Who is he? I had recovered enough by now to think about more than just me. Is it Guards?

Oh, please can it be Guards.

No, it wasn't even one Guard. It was a College security man.

"Call an ambulance," I agreed finally with my wife. Next, I sensed the square yellow cab squeezing past my open door. Somehow the paramedics got me out, without mishap you will be pleased to learn, and began to do things.

"We are going to take him to hospital, his blood pressure is very low." Those were the last words I remember until the bumping over uneven surfaces stopped and the siren was turned off. And then peace.

Do you know, I am sick to death – hah! – sick *nearly* to death of hearing people complaining about this in hospital or that in hospital. I think it's all pretty good – and I have spent night after night on trolleys and eaten hospital food for month upon month. If I could wave a magic wand at one thing, however, it would be at the rear suspension of our ambulances. It is terrible. (The background silence was suddenly deafening: it was as if everything round the backdoor of A&E was listening for my reaction. Spot on boyo, the breeze seemed to whisper.) As an old Highland friend of mine, who frequently hitched a lift to the bar at the nearby hotel in the back of the community hearse but now found himself admitted by ambulance for more serious reasons to his regional hospital, told me when I visited him: "Even a corp gets a better ride." A wheelchair in the corner began to shake, apparently in amusement, until one of its foot plates fell off.

My wife joined me having followed in the jeep and parked it somewhere. Silence. Calm. The doctors sat at a table somewhere on the left. What was the point of being here, I wondered? But I no longer had any answers. So, I just waited to see what would happen.

And then it started.

First, my left cheek felt odd. Distinctly leathery. Next, slight pins and needles on the outside of my left foot … and then in my left palm. Funny, I thought. I waited to see if the sensations would go away. But they didn't. Bells began to sound – something I read years ago. *Oh, no!*

"I'm having a stroke! Tell them, darling, *tell them that I'm having a stroke*," I repeated this, shouting it even, until they promised to take me for a CAT scan. Keep the old duffer quiet, they must have been thinking. For my part, I thanked God a fourth time, that today A&E (or ERD as they seem to call it now) was enjoying a quiet afternoon. A second CAT scan later and the medical staff all agreed that the signs were pointing towards a stroke. A doctor explained the risks of the essential medicine and that time was precious. I thought I had been pretty quick in my reactions, quicker even than the A&E staff, but my contribution seemed to have been forgotten about by the time he stuck the needle in. Never mind, I simply notched up the silent victory.

And that, truthfully, is the last clear recollection he had in his first five weeks in the acute stroke unit of Cork University Hospital and of his most spectacular entrance. Images, yes. Moments of annoyance and of gratitude; of gentle handling and extreme kindness. But clear, coherent passages of time and for observation, no.

On one occasion, he did remember apologising to someone with a proud, distinguished African face because this dark visitor had to clean him twice in the space of an hour. The face looked at him for a moment and then said: "Don't be embarrassed," his voice was educated, "this is our job. This is what we do. We clean people who cannot do it for themselves."

There was such gentleness in his manner, such kindness, that the occupant of the wheelchair, which was where he now sat, began to cry. People who have had a stroke do cry readily. I think he was crying for the nobility in his face, this impressive immigrant who cleaned people up when they couldn't do it for themselves. Where did he come from, this gentle prince who calmed me and loved me by holding me and my distress in his outstretched arms?

Don't forget about me, whispered the wheelchair.

I met this African prince about a year later when I had been readmitted for something related. I was lying on a trolley in the same old A&E department when a ward assistant (or whatever the correct title is) walked past and looked my way. He soon came back with a wheelchair and our eyes met – it was him.

"Hello," I said, speaking from the trolley "it's you, isn't it."

It turned out that he had been re-appointed from the third floor to the ground, to the emergency area. We went for a shower for old time's sake (at that point I couldn't walk) and which I needed after a night on a trolley in my day clothes. I won't say my African friend's name in order to protect him but we certainly had great *craic*. It seems the face came from South Africa and – you'll love this bit, said the wheelchair which by now was rather wet – he was an accountant. We pay him to wash backsides and he's an accountant. Enough said.

And what about me? muttered the wheelchair. I did my Leaving[2], you know.

---

[2] The Leaving Certificate, or 'Leaving', is the daunting, final examination at school or second level in Ireland. Once accomplished, many students will try to obtain a place at third

In the fourth week of my long admission last year, that was in March 2019, a structure began to shape the passing days, so we'll pick up the story there.

Physiotherapy. Or more accurately: "Physio this afternoon!" This normally meant that I would be ready in the wheelchair from about the start of *Liveline* on RTE Radio One. I disliked - sorr*ee*, I changed direction quickly – I was *concerned for* the wheelchair because bits kept falling off (it was always the same wheelchair, it never changed: what have I done, I thought, to upset the Controller of Wheelchairs so seriously? The wheelchair trembled ominously beside the bed and finally

---

level, sufficient 'leaving' points permitting. To be able to declare that one had completed 'the Leaving' was like a badge of competence and intellectual endorsement. Not to have completed 'the Leaving' was ... well, one didn't mention it.

the left foot plate thudded to the floor again). A porter would turn up at any time from lunchtime until mid-afternoon and then we would set off; sometimes the journey would be extended as we retraced our steps looking for a missing bit; but mainly, the journey passed uneventfully. Occasionally, however, the outing to the gym would be postponed altogether until the following day.

Quite where this flexible approach to time-keeping originated, I was neither sure nor concerned enough to find out: the porters, who had more calls on their services than I could imagine, were always smart, courteous and good company; and the physio team and their patients could be relied upon to extend a genuinely warm welcome and to make immediate space for latecomers and unexpected joiners at one or other piece of equipment around the gymnasium walls. Of course, I may have got the whole thing wrong as my poor, damaged mind struggled to regain its sense of where I was and of what I was doing – and of that priceless commodity, time. All I could confidently say is that my condition – *I don't have a condition!* came a new voice inside me – my condition, the rational part of me insisted, began to improve in their care. The wheelchair grumbled that he had a condition too but only I could hear. So, I ignored it.

It was on one of these daily adventures, from the third-floor ward to the ground floor gym, that it was suddenly brought home to me how lucky I had been. While waiting to be collected by a porter, my wheelchair was parked next to someone whose bed had been opposite mine on the ward for a few days.

I had noticed that I was younger than the patient opposite who had a very attentive family. *Over*-attentive, I had already decided dismissively. But then, down there in the gym, the reason for their energy and their focus suddenly became clear. My task in the gymnasium that day had been walking between parallel bars, practising my balance – and I was feeling pretty good about myself, having shuffled 30 meters without falling over, and 30 meters back. The other patient, in comparison, was picking up small, wooden pegs from a tray beside him and fitting them into holes in another tray on his lap – and, from what the occupant of the wheelchair could tell, he wasn't doing very well.

His brain had been damaged whereas the occupant of the wheelchair … let's stop this as it's getting confusing. Me, I had escaped by the tiniest fraction of an inch and could still walk and think. God, I have been lucky. The wheelchair seemed to sniff and whisper: what about the wife, he asked, what about the wife?

And, yes, what about that family as opposed to mine? Their's was never over-attention. It was love. Love spilling for the person they had lost. Love desperately trying to claw back something from the disaster. Love trying to keep something afloat from the lifeless body sinking before their eyes. At last, they all understood what he had seen from the wheelchair and from the bed opposite in the dying light of the day: Rachel weeping for her children, refusing to be comforted[3].

There were times, during those few weeks, in the quiet moments after evening visiting hours and before lights out, that he regularly noticed a Rachel, silently bent over one or other a

---

[3] St Matthew 2:18 "A voice is heard in Ramah, crying and great mourning... [it was Rachel weeping for her children]."

bedside in the ward, even his own faithful Rachel bending over his own.

Widening his thoughts, he began to understand rather more, too, about Ireland's own 19th century famines and what they must have done to rural families. The sad sepia prints and paintings hanging on the chipped plaster walls began to make more sense. There were some on the walls around him. Why had it taken a wheelchair on the third floor to enable him to step inside their landscape of pain? Could it possibly travel through space and through time?

He began to take an interest in differences between his ward-mates and himself. It surprised him how many had been by themselves when their strokes hit. Had they known what was happening to them? Did they shout out loud as he had done? Had there been anyone there to hear? He began to look at notice boards as well. FAST, they said. Someone is having a stroke they said, so *Act FAST*. The word was everywhere but how useful was it?

FACE … ARM … SPEECH … TIME …Well, he could only claim that one of those had applied in his case: the first one, his face. He began to wonder if the general idea of reacting quickly to prescribed, visible clues was a bit fanciful. Obviously something had alerted him to a change in his face while lying in A&E, but it wasn't a leaflet or a message, and only on touching his cheek did he realise that it felt leathery. No-one looking at him would have detected any change at all. And he hadn't been following any acronym when he began to shout for help in A&E.

Dear me, he thought, have we been putting out the wrong message? Having nothing better to do, he set about testing the notion.

"Does my cheek look odd?" he asked one of the nurses several weeks later when it still felt exactly the same as the night my stroke occurred. According to FAST, something should have been visible by then, if not much earlier.

"No it looks fine," she replied .

Well. That meant to him that any victim of stroke could have long since run out of time for any FAST effective responses based on how his or her face looked. Following his reasoning, ARM wasn't much use either – it would have been within a day or two of his own stroke but not on the night in question. Exactly the same went for SPEECH. So, who was FAST directed at?

Whom, interjected his wheelchair which, despite being loosely assembled, seemed somewhat fastidious when it came to things like grammar.

Whom, he continued. And how effective was it? Not having access to data – and not knowing what data actually existed anyway – he could only focus on what was around him.

Him?

It's me I am talking about.

And what was around me was mostly elderly men who had been by themselves when the stroke struck or in a situation where they and their immediate surroundings had closed down for the night. So, whom – *who* could possibly have been alert to changes in their physiology but themselves?

Only themselves, I thought. And their respective Rachels ...

I began to ponder male dependence upon womenfolk and weaker partners, upon where strength lay in any partnership, on how long such partnerships last and upon undemanding love and care even beyond that of my African prince. But I had no answers to such mysteries.

Helpfully, our wheelchair-taxi arrived outside the large glass window and swung round the small roundabout into a designated space. Soon we were on board and ready. No more 'physio this afternoon'. It was '*Re*-hab now!' And we were off.

Cork has many old back streets which have long since seen their best. Their condition is poor whichever route is chosen. And that is half the appeal: there are so many different ways to any given destination that one can never be entirely sure which one the driver has decided to follow before you actually set off. It gives you different things to talk about and reminds you of the parts you irregularly visit. But some things never change – the broadly comparable time needed to get from A to B whatever the route taken, and the condition of the roads and their unsuitability for the amount and size of today's traffic, again whatever the route taken. So there is always a mixed measure of entertainment and achievement on completing a journey without incident and yet still predictably at the time you knew you would arrive.

It turned up *en route* that the wheelchair came from the southside of the city. It could be heard sniffing as the driver crossed the river and followed the northern quays. I had learned by now to ignore such interruptions and the wheelchair soon shut up. Anyway, we were by then on the southside. I can think of shorter routes, muttered the wheelchair in tones that apparently only I could hear. And then: How much is this costing?

Eventually we arrived at *Re*-hab where the porter scribbled his signature. Cost was not going to be an issue. But having begun in a coma, I had no sense of where we had started from and therefore how long we'd been driving. I really need to stress this observation for it is cruelly relevant in understanding my wider case: I personally have no sense of origin, none at all. The point will re-occur and is largely what this story is about: large scale, small scale, I have no sense of where I came from in either context. The wheelchair tactfully stayed silent.

Not having come from anywhere there between the Cork University Hospital and St Finbarre's Hospital, I could not share the Corkman's sense of certainty, back and consequently forwards. I knew the routes alright but not the corners, I knew the sounds and signs and stopping places but I didn't know the dialect of each successive step and stumble. I knew the accent but that was all. And not having a sense of origin, how do you measure when and how the voices are changing and which direction you are going in?

That sentence is so important that I shall repeat its essentials. If you don't know where you come from, how do you know where you are going? You can judge where *they* are going – him, and him, and her, and the wheelchair – each on their different routes passing busily and pre-occupiedly by as their life unfolds before them, but how are you safely to imitate? To isolate and reproduce? And if you cannot separate out the pavements and the safe walks, the lawns and the quays behind me, how are you to measure the distances you still have to go? How are you ever confidently to say "This way. Follow me. You are safe now." And if you cannot attract any followers, then how exemplary will your life seem … to anyone?

And this is the next very important point. If you don't know where you have come from – and now the important bit – at what point will you be able to say anything useful … about anything? Even to a bold taximan: You are trying to charge me too much!

(The academic in me – oh God, yawned the wheelchair disrespectfully – knows that answers lie in operationalising the routes, corners, dialects and accents. A foot plate fell dramatically to the floor. Are we any the wiser, its echo seemed to ask.)

There appear to be three issues – places, actions and words. So, how would I make my impact through places, actions and words? My poor old life, cluttered up with fallen bits and limping wheelchairs, with crisis-ridden families whom I could only look at and wonder why, was of no interest to anyone, it occurred to me, because of this one pervasive truth. It seemed to get in the way of everything. Why is their tragedy so virtuous and heroic and mine so incidental, so much less worthy of *Re*-hab than theirs? It was because, unlike them, I never had an answer at all to that one essential, recurring question: "Now, tell me, boy, where do you come from?"

(To be called 'boy', or rather 'bye', is pure Cork. Take care to listen to how it is pronounced: this can range from affection to a declaration of war. Two further comments may be helpful. First, you could not wish to find better people than pure Corkonians. They are straight and direct in what they say and how they say it – which is another way of saying 'listen very carefully'. And second, local variations in pronunciation of the simple monosyllable 'boy' may – I stress 'may' – owe their roots to the Irish word for 'boy', *buachaill*. This can be swallowed, smoothed and generally rounded in many different ways between the lips of the expert *gaeilgeoir* and could possibly, just possibly, explain how the City of Cork came to adopt the word.)

Time to get out, biy, muttered the wheelchair kindly. Stop your theorising, we have arrived.

But where were they going to *Re*-hab me to? I still didn't know and clawed desperately at the inside of my consciousness as they wheeled me through the bottom door of my new ward. If I don't know where I started from, who gives you the right to decide where I should next be sent? And who with? (Did someone whisper 'whom'?) I shouted this, or something like it, as they wheeled me through the bottom door and into one of the single-bed sidewards. Coma was thus replaced by a sense of ungrammatical outrage, which was probably one planned step along the way. Suddenly, I was alone and isolation brings unusual thoughts.

Stupid old duffer, I think I heard someone say nearby. What an eejit, I thought in agreement and turned my mind to those other things.

We think of rivers starting as a single stream, then growing in width and depth, and finally spreading out into an estuary – a place of differentiation, of multi-flows, some shallow, some tidal, but all spreading out as the character of the water's edge changes and multiplies before reaching the open sea. *Les bouches du Rhône*, I remembered from happier times in Provence in the south of France.

"Where are you from?"

"My family has lived up there by the start of the stream for many generations," comes the reply. *Fons,* as our Latin-educated forebears might have put it. Source, beginning. (Clutching at half-remembered Latin nouns seemed, briefly, a useful mental exercise.)

"Where are *you* from?"

"I come from that valley up there, by the bank of the river," comes a different reply. *Genus,* a family, a closely related species dwelling in more productive ground further down the flow.

"And where are you from, bye?"

"That ship out there. We dropped anchor yesterday We are just sailing by." *Ag dul ó áit go háit*, as they might say in Irish. *Ar fad*, whispered the wheelchair. I spent half my life just sailing by, collecting phrases like that, seeking tides which lead God knows where. The poet Byron said something similar knowing that the most you can construe is that people who lead their lives in the way I am describing do indeed have little sense of origin and certainly none up either bank of the next passing river. I have also found that having no sense of origin adds an air of mystery: it postpones briefly and privatises undoubtedly the inevitable sense of isolation. *Regardez-le... ... un 'ricochet'... ... pah!* Oh for someone, just once, to say:

Regardez-nous, deux plantes ensembles. That word 'together'. Just once please.

"D'accord", agreed the wheelchair who obviously spoke French as well as Irish. But that was the most the thing would say.

So, isolated yet again, until they found a permanent bed for me, I returned to the question of where they were going to finally *Re*-hab me to. Don't forget me, came a final observation from the wheelchair and then, in a cockney accent, I'm stuck 'ere too – signed out I am and you're responsible. Goodness, I thought, to be responsible seemed mightily impressive. But for whom – for him or for me? 'Both' was a concept just too far at that point in time.

In the days before digital navigation, you could work out where you had come from by dint of neat and accurate chartwork. By maintaining a careful passage plan and preserving a record of the navigational track, almost everything is clear. The word 'almost' contains the key: you can work back to a given port's point of departure but what happened up to then?

"Where did you come from before that?" And if you can't come up with an answer, I wondered, how would they agree some earlier point for *Re*-hab? You see, there is nothing at sea, just waves, wistfulness and memories over the horizon. And, of course, a looming sense of the next port of arrival. This mysterious place 'hab', where they were proposing to send you back to, was nowhere in sight. You can't impose *Re*-hab on someone if you cannot define or describe 'hab', I theorised to no-one in particular. You just can't.

Alright, I take the point, muttered something eventually, in the corner.

As my eyes roved around my new room, exploring those corners and learning where their secrets were and what they might entail, I rehearsed my own particular history anticipating the clipboards and questions of the laid down induction process:

Born in a country which doesn't exist anymore (because they changed its name, character and legal personality). Born in a house which doesn't exist anymore (because a *tsu-nami* demolished it). Lived in 43 different homes by the time I had reached that age (because mobility and a parent's career and interests were deemed more important than childhood stability and, despite maturity, I never quite lost the habit of regular uprooting). Six schools only one of which I liked, loved so much that the pain of leaving is still there many decades later. More of this to come. Much more.

An audible yawn came from the same corner of the room where the wheelchair had been abandoned.

Five countries lived in, I continued. No friends of my own, and only friends of my parents plus a load of their memories. Don't get me wrong, I broke into the self-pity: I actually liked their friends. Quite simply, my parents followed their own fork as they worked their way down to the sea and took me with them. Leaving me with no footsteps in the sand, with neither camouflage nor compass whatsoever and just their own track to follow. Dragged.

"Where's the *fons* and *genus* in all that?" I asked out loud.

In your inner strength and resilience, came an unspoken reply.

Is that you? I called to the wheelchair. But nothing, I could hear nothing. It wasn't the wheelchair which seemed to be sulking in silence. I noticed that one of its tyres had deflated.

"So, where are they going to *Re*-hab me to?" I persisted in the other conversation.

Wait and see, was the answer. Then puzzlingly: *You have already reached it; you have done your Re-hab but don't let them know; you don't recognise it because your brain is damaged but you are stronger than any of them; just sit back now and watch and think and remember. Just enjoy the ride.*

The wheelchair smirked but still said nothing, sitting quietly with its flat tyre. It looked like one great, lopsided grin. Something like an overgrown bullfrog although I don't recall ever seeing even an ordinary-sized one. Bullfrog, I muttered. Bollocks, the wheelchair spat back.

It was impossible to sleep, so new and puzzling were the sounds and interruptions. I did manage to identify the sound of an air pump amongst them but it didn't last long. Over- ... grown ... indeed ... , it seemed to croak in successive, noisy, froggy pumps.

Later I discovered that, for some people, the old buildings were – well, were difficult to be in alone. It was a consequence of their former use, it seemed. A workhouse. A place for people who owed no real debt to society but whom society was going to inflict misery upon if they couldn't pay on time. Not paying on time? Not being on time or some other trivial misdemeanour like enjoying the surge of new life in their limbs and between them. Dear God, what did society do to such poor souls that the plaster on the walls still screams out their despair?

I have this theory that walls, being the means of confinement, absorb pain. Like *La Conciergerie,* in Paris, where poor souls destined for *la guillotine* were herded, shrieking when their time came. Similarly, Lara Marlowe, writing for *The Irish Times* in December 2020, also records the belief of the Senior Architect consulting over the rebuilding of the cathedral of nearby *Notre Dame* that the prayers of the faithful were literally "encrusted" in the walls. I certainly felt the sadness in the walls at St Finbarre's that first night in *Re*-hab.

Please God, don't keep me here.

Stay there. Don't be afraid.

Surely I began in a happier place.

Stay here.

Here?

Where are you? I asked but no-one replied. .

I remembered pictures of fine beaches, of basins and tanks (as they called them) of salt water where crocodiles might lurk, lifeless apparently, below the surface waiting for the incautious; where herds of holy elephants waded in safe places and frightened them away. Could I not please *Re*-hab there? Leave me out of this, said the wheelchair.

I thought of compounds, designed to keep the pi-dogs out and even leopard whose breathing sent a terrifying sawing sound through the jungle night. But it didn't keep everything out. I didn't mind, I was always intrigued by the things that squeezed through the wire. Please could you *Re*-hab me back there? "*Re*-hab! There!" I shouted. "Not here, where I don't belong." A footplate fell noisily off the wheelchair.

"Look, Nanny! Krait. Krait!" I cried out the alarm in the compound where I did once, briefly belong. It had somehow squeezed through and turned the compound into a place of exclamation marks. Nanny told them all about my courage and the dangerous snake before she went to Government house! I have more old photographs of Nanny holding me than I do of my mother doing the same! In sad fact, there is only one of the latter and I don't remember any other instance of it either … !

That was the only picture I am certain now. I don't ever recall her picking me up or holding me, even in the following years. She even shuddered when I embraced her on visits before I fell ill. Ninety-seven years when I last saw her and she still shuddered at the touch of me. I have washed filth off her and cared for her but she shudders at me …

There is one picture of her standing alone wearing a swimsuit as they quaintly called them then, while Nanny habitually wore a long sarong, colourful, graceful, with a simple blouse. I could pick her out from old sepia photographs of all the nannies in an arc, their charges crawling around on the ground in front of them as if they had squeezed through the wire, too. Nanny's skirt swayed and her oiled hair shone perfectly black, as she departed on her way to Government House. God, my mother was so proud ...

God, someone's priorities were wrong even then. Don't involve me in this, the wheelchair appeared to be thinking.

Nanny went on her way there, skipping over me as over the krait, an unwanted risk better left alone and behind. Like litter, although I don't think she felt like that. There is another photograph of me with a sawn-off walking stick and flat hat, like an already half-old man limping along before his time, abandoned on some well-kept lawn. Even then, I noticed in the picture, there was something with wheels on beside me. Hobbling along with my broken toy I was content, but they didn't leave me there. And now I cannot even limp and all

I've got is this wheelchair –

Ayup! came an interjection of alarm from the corner in an unfamiliar Yorkshire accent, which again I chose to ignore. (The accent must have come with the hat and the walking stick.) We are now both decrepit before our time, I continued courageously. Easy, lad, easy, muttered the wheelchair in still rising concern. And then, confusingly, in a spitting Welsh valleys accent: speak for yourself, bhoyo, speak for yourself. I ignored the repeated interruptions and the rapid geolinguistic variations bravely, feeling nearer the point I was trying to make.

I shall probably depart this world at least a decade before my father did (92 years old on passing, may he rest in peace), and will probably not last as long as my mother (presently ninety-eight years old and heading strongly for a century). Good Lord, I might actually predecease her – I am certainly out of favour and would scarcely be missed. In fact, when I come to think about it, nothing about my life seems to have followed the customarily pre-ordained plans; I have nearly always been out of favour; my existence has never really been 'in synch' with my soul, with myself, with my psyche or with worldly expectations like those of my family such as it was. Do people see two figures when they look at me? Or a fractured group? Or simply a shadow, captured crumbling in the cracks upon the wall? Perhaps my mark is in the wall already.

Quite interesting, I thought in the silence of the night and the heavy breathing from the corner. There must be other shadows, too. The thoughts that circled around me were emphatically not an example of self-pity: I was … I *am* genuinely trying to analyse myself in order that anything I might say in the following pages which is useful or, sufficiently entertaining to be memorable, can be separated out from unwanted influences arising from my residual, emotional muddle. Muddle? Turmoil.

That's an unnecessary and very long sentence, commented the wheelchair at last breaking its self-imposed silence but with its eyes firmly shut. There is nothing unnecessary and unwanted over 'ere, I can tell you.

I tried to break it up …

What did I try to break up? Not the sentence, surely? I wondered, reading back two weeks after I had written the phrase. Never mind. I have forgotten what I was going to say. I seem to forget quite a lot since the stroke but, by and large, the missing thoughts seem to catch up. It's a bit like thoughts connected like children's toy railway carriages which suddenly arrive in a sequence of harmless shunts somewhere behind my left ear. Some get lost en route, God knows where, and finally muddle themselves in with the rest of the mental décor.

Anyway, we all settled down, the wheelchair, me and the various whispers, spirits and shadows in my side room. We slept until morning, me in my half awareness and them, disturbed no longer, just dreaming their own pain and memories away as the clock ticked silently past the hours. And so I learned the first truth about *Re*-hab: time passes. It may pass slowly and sometimes fast, but whatever its pace and whoever is controlling it, time will pass.

The second truth was rather more prosaic.

"Where are the bells!" a woman's voice cried "There are no bells!" As a new staff nurse was being shown around the ward in the early hours of the morning, she explained that six months in the adjacent female ward had accustomed her to the constant calling of bells – to pick up this which had been dropped or to collect something else which had been forgotten. Nothing, it seemed, to do with nursing. Men in *Re*-hab, I was told, were so much easier. The words floated over her shoulder as I compared this revelation with my faithful wife who, undeservedly and without complaint, had trudged repeatedly through snow and rain to bring me things each time I was inside: "*So* much easier …" trailed the receding voice from up the corridor.

Some months later I learned the hard way about the needs and demands of female patients. I'm sorry, ladies, but here is the truth. I have to get it out. It's blocking everything else, the light and even my breath.

I had been re-admitted following something arrhythmic which wasn't but might have been, an invisible punch in the chest that was briefly terrifying given my post severe stroke status. I was lying with others in a 'men only' corridor of A&E, all of us quietly prone upon our trolleys waiting for a bed. And then a lady about the same age as me was brought in in the middle of the night and her trolley was pushed in just ahead of mine. She called for the nurse so often that the A&E staff vacated the area completely and because I couldn't stand her screaming, I got up myself, with my arrhythmia, my stroke, and my recent punch in the chest, and eventually found a nurse. It really pained me but I did manage to get back to my trolley hobbling from wall to wall without falling over. In fact, I didn't mind because they took the old dear to the loo which evidently she needed badly. But within a minute or two of her being tucked up again on her trolley, the screaming started once more. I am not exaggerating. (He doesn't, came helpful support from the wheelchair.) In desperation, I eventually struggled up once more and went to look for one of the nurses who by this time were hiding from the resumed yelling down the corridor. Once I had found a nurse (I think she was hiding in the sluice), she overtook me on the way back. But I was close enough to hear this old biddy on the trolley ask the nurse to adjust her

67

pillow-height. That was all she had been screaming for: *to adjust her pillow height.* And then out she hops, I notice, as I struggle back, without any evidence of anything wrong. She did have something wrong with her, however, when both the nurse and I had given her the rough edge of our tongues.

And here's the twist. She then starts screaming "I'm sorry, I'm sorry" until I have to get out of bed again to find a nurse to make her shut up. Oh dear, my heart was pumping 'til it nearly broke.

Oh my good Gawd, came a vulgar interruption from somewhere down the corridor.

How did the wheelchair get down there, I wondered in response.

new phrase entered the lexicon: 'mood-lifting'. Please pay careful attention: mood-lifting.

It seemed that someone had dreamed up a cloud of damaging depression hanging around my bed. Yes, they agreed, he needs an antidepressant. I didn't agree but my voice counted for nothing. I learned pretty quickly that the only way to resist such medicine is to assert, and keep asserting, that they have already had an unpleasant side-effect. In other words, you tell them that you have tried such pills already and the experience was not good. You lie. But not knowing the value at the time of this paradox, I walked straight into the trap and took a pill. The wheelchair stayed silent, made sure its brakes were on and watched developments.

Whether I took another pill the second day, I cannot be certain but I am quite sure that the side-effects lasted three nights. Indeed, I still experienced the images ten months later and *still believe there is more to come –*

Twenty two months and counting, biy, came the correction from the clock in the corner which now wore two big wheels, two small and one big smirk. He's right: it's November 2020, twenty to twenty two months after probably first taking them, and I had another 'experience' last night; details to follow later.

I can see these images, even now, in a clear enough form to find them severely disturbing. I am telling you this so that you can avoid these tablets. I still experience the effects more than a year later and may yet endure them in the years ahead. I urge you to refuse these drugs, to categorically reject the notion that your mood needs external stimulus.

Don't do it. These things are dangerous. Here, judge for yourself.

At some point, I was moved to a larger ward which seemed to be housed in a spacious camouflaged tent. The floor was grass and the occupant of the bed opposite me had come from the main ward in the hospital to this *Re-*hab centre, so we knew each other. And then they discharged him just when I had found some comfort in his proximity. Welcome companionship but they sent him home, together with the people on each side. And so the night started with three empty beds. Three empty beds opposite mine. In a large camouflaged tent. With grass on the floor.

One bed filled up quite quickly and a visitor came calling on the new arrival. He was alright, the person in the bed, but his visitor began prowling around. This visitor had slicked down short-cut hair with an awkward high-cut hairline, and was wearing a tightly buttoned, flannel, grey suit which I didn't like. It looked baggy and old-fashioned.: 1940s, turn-ups and with extravagant flaps, lapels and turn-ups. He was under-weight and the suit was cut for someone larger and yet it still looked tightly buttoned. Still flapping slightly on his spare frame, malnourished I thought, the suit looked shabby as well. He explored lockers and containers but also investigated those belonging to other patients on the opposite side of the ward. Things he had no right to look in.

I didn't like his manner either and was terrified lest he came over to my bedside. Even the person he was visiting looked distinctly uncomfortable at what was happening. And then this unwelcome visitor, wearing round metal-rimmed glasses, said he was leaving but would return later. "What time do they switch the lights off?" "Nine thirty." "I'll be back at a quarter to 10," he announced as he slipped out of the tent.

Oh Jaysus.

That was the dream on the first night and it filled a good number of hours, even though he never came back that night. But ten months later, yes, nearly a year after taking that pill, when I was back in my room at home, I found myself once more in that same field ward. He returned and occupied the bed beside me. He came back. Oh God, no.

No! *No!*

He kept reaching over for the clinical file hanging at the bottom of my bed. *My* bed.

And then he started writing things, *in my file,* where doctors only wrote! *Oh God, won't someone stop him?* But I got him. I managed to reach him and I dragged him over to my bed where I gave him a right bating … we ended up on the floor where I bate the daylights out of the nearby sofa. I bate it until I woke up lying on the floor, bleeding, bruised and with the upholstery all spoiled and scattered around me. I am always bleeding because of the blood-thinners but this time it was worse. It was the second time I had cried since that man in the other hospital helped me. Now I had given myself more wounds than was fair. But at least the man had gone.

The first time I cried … well, I think I mentioned that already.

If my bleeding over the arm of an upholstered sofa were not enough, the dream itself still did not completely switch itself off all those months earlier when I first took the pill. An alarm sounded at some point but I appeared to be the only one to respond. Was this still my dream or were we back in the real world? Still not knowing, I responded to the alarm by managing to get up and out of my bed in which time the unpleasant visitor managed to disappear leaving his promise to return, drifting still audible, in the draught like unpleasant, nauseous cigarette smoke. It seemed that we were now waiting to get on an aeroplane which would take us away and out of the area and, therefore, served as a welcome distraction from his Gestapo-like menace. Furthermore, I was an aviator having spent 19 years flying helicopters at sea. So, my mood improved immediately (if it was ever down in the first place, before taking the blessed pill).

Do you now begin to see what a time-muddled mess these drugs create?

Quite how I got from the ward to the aeroplane I do not know. Similarly, I don't know how I recovered sufficiently to be standing in the hold of a World War II aeroplane, holding on to the upright bars on either side of the open, sliding doorway. But I am quite clear that I was watching a long line of civilian refugees running along a ditch across the end of the airfield, just behind the aeroplane itself. Running in terror. I remember waving them urgently in towards the tented ward which lay round to my left out of sight in the corner of the airfield – the same tented ward that I had earlier lain sick inside. Somehow, my dream-logic told me, the refugees would be vetted and cleared in the tent and then brought out to the aeroplane where I would make them safe.

Was any of this frightening? Well, the refugees were frightened and the unpleasant visitor was frightening. But, as for the rest, not really at the time except that there was a coherence across this historical picture that smoothed out the disruption caused by daylight and the work of the various *Re*-hab wards and left something unsettling in its place. Wherever my dream had reached in the early morning, it started again at that same particular point the next following night. And then it kept coming regardless of the interruption of the daylight hours. That became quite scary. Particularly when I noticed that those running, trying to run, were increasingly weak and poorly clothed. It was their clothing that alerted me to what I was actually observing. Their clothing ... ragged clothing ...

Furthermore, the sensation of evil attaching to the visitor to the patient in the bed opposite mine began to strengthen, although I never saw him again while I was in R*e*-hab. And that was unpleasant, too. Something unpleasant behind me. Behind me in time but could re-emerge, as it has, out there in front. This was something I could for the first time be certain about. And then there was the sensation that we ('we'? No, you. This 'we' 'ad nuffin' to do with it, contributed the wheelchair) – *I* ... I was not on a film set but living a life somewhere behind lines, waiting to be rescued, during World War II. Living a real life and now needing to escape as quickly as we could. It was something to do with their clothing ... It was striped and dirty.

Striped and dirty ...

I had no doubt in my mind, no doubt whatsoever, that they had come from a concentration camp.

But there was something else, too.

The real-life structure of the ward was of a long corridor with small wards off, all on one side. That basic shape continued into my night-time experience. But then, as the weeks passed, it began to creep into, to populate, the day-time shape and activities within the ward. And in so doing, the space of the corridor began to assume a different character. There was an iron beam that passed overhead along the length of the corridor: that became the main spar of the wing section. Smaller beams became supporting struts and the few ward spaces became stowages for the sick and for life jackets. I never quite found the route to the cockpit but I did repeatedly warn the startled ward staff that I was worried about the payload and its distribution. And I recall conducting a daily conversation on the topic with the senior physiotherapist who came to collect me and take me down to the gym. I pointed out the different features of the wing spar and struts. Oh dear. He must have thought me utterly mad but I also made sure to tell as many people as I could that I couldn't tolerate these awful, dangerous mood-lifting drugs. That and that everyone was to help the people running from the camp … I imagine someone will have been concerned enough to put it in my notes. I wonder what they wrote?

I kept turning left out of the ward, too, because I was frightened at the weight distribution. I wouldn't go back the other way until led, reassured, by a member of staff away to the right towards the gymnasium. I am sure they'll have put that in the records somewhere, that I would never turn right. And there was also a voice I could hear in the gymnasium – high up in the far corner on the right as you go in. I had never heard 'an unholy scream' before. That won't be in the records, I didn't tell them that. I am sorry – I did. I told one of the physios and she looked scared but I didn't want to frighten anyone so I didn't say anything else after that.

Oh dear. All very upsetting.

They tried to give me a different drug while still in the main hospital. But that made me see a woman patient in the bed opposite mine, in a men-only ward, twisting and turning and making extraordinary silhouette shapes with her hands. And then I realised that there was a man hidden in her bed clothes who could also do 'magic'. You could see bits of him and then bits of her. Some performance, I can tell you. Nothing obscene, just bizarre, amazing and downright odd. It went on for several days, too, until my mind began to unscramble. And then her son came to apologise but I didn't know what for. Perhaps he was part of their trickery?

As I said, don't take these pills unless you really have to.

The next truth was that wherever you joined a group of patients – in a side ward, for example – however pleasant and agreeable the group might be, someone, some new patient, would soon be introduced to the group who would wreck the peace, calm and equilibrium. Perhaps I had been the guilty one for them? I tried not be, especially when noticing a small 'cell' which looked better-stocked with *poitín* in their corner of the ward than I recall seeing in my two previous decades of life on a Munster suckler farm. Such cells can be dangerous if exposed, so I always looked the other way whenever the *buidéal* was brought out. And in looking the other way, so the impression must have grown that I really hadn't noticed their secret at all. It was a bit like Compton MacKenzie's delightful book 'Whisky Galore' where they named contraband Scotch whisky 'Minnie' so as not to raise suspicion. Well, in my ward, they had a similar name for the *poitín* and, do you know, the more they referred to the wonderful stuff by this name, the more they drank it. They appeared to get reckless. Or was it the other way round?

Whatever, they must have thought I was born yesterday – either that or they had such a drunk on them which overcame all sense of where they were and what they were meant to be doing. Anyway, I kept their secret and eventually went on my way, relieved to be out of their company and clear of a gathering storm cloud.

And that's another truth. Don't upset the ward staff. They are fantastic people doing a pretty mucky and essential job, and don't deserve being messed around. There was one lady who washed the floors and cleaned the loos and worse. Eventually, I managed tactfully to engage her on the subject of her job. Why did she do it?

"I like talking to the patients," came the reply. Her face lit up. Her voice changed from lazy-Cork to well-spoken-Cork. And she smiled the sweetest smile imaginable. I tell you I was no longer a cocky University-educated blow-in but a very humble human being who had just been fortunate enough to talk to a real live angel.

A prince one week and an angel the next. Goodness me, where was I going?

Round and round, came a familiar voice from the corner. In something like a kaleidoscope world, I continued ignoring the interruption.

Re-hab was an immediate change from the hospital ward. If something needed to be done, domestic things, they would bring you the tools and materials and then stand back. Believe me, said the wheelchair, I can stand back longer than you can. And of course the wheelchair was right: after a brief struggle with myself, I took up the tools and tried to do whatever it was myself.

A spoon, a knife and a fork was the starting point. Oh God, you should hae seen yon mess –

"*have* seen *the* mess," interrupted a passing starched bosom. I ducked my head, said nothing and looked awa'.

I recalled being up the hill behind our small town along the Hillfoot line in Scotland. They called it 'the Hillfoots' because the villages and small towns lined the southern edge of the Scottish Highlands: the lowest slope of the hillside started among the houses. It was very noticeable by our house where a burn tumbled down, icy cold and full of trout if only small ones. The road was called Burnside, just to make it clear to visitors who hadn't understood or didn't care like we did. Oh God, how did we care. We all loved that place with its little stone footbridges over the rocks and foaming water from East to West Burnside. And behind our house was the most magnificent school and palladian building. I went to my class up the garden path, over the fence and down the grass slope to a nearby door. And then, one day, it burned down. The school. It wasn't me. It wasn't anyone. It was just a fault in the wiring. But it was a total disaster for life in that particular mountain range and in the remainder of mine.

I stared through my side-ward window at the grass slope outside but, compared with my beloved highland home, only a drab, prefabricated, single story, brick shape was in sight. Isn't memory a wonderful thing that it can so lift the spirits and take you where you will? Take you somewhere else? The downside of course is that each flight of fancy releases a shot of pain we call nostalgia. And that is because we don't think enough about what is happening or where we're heading: we let the nostalgia 'hit' us a moment or two before we are ready for it and in places we don't want to be hit. And that, in turn, is because we have allowed ourselves to become lazy.

I pondered these grand, judgemental thoughts lying, ga-ga, on my bed with serious pain up my left-hand side and into the back of my head. At the time it was a steady pain but later it became like electric shocks which came down the arm rather than travelling up. And then spasms. Violent jerks. Where were they going to, I wondered. I returned to my theorising of nostalgia in order to distract myself. My left arm was still twitching involuntarily. I needed to distract myself, to travel back and remember. I needed to have the door of my little 'sub-ward' shut in case any visitor saw me. Oh please don't let any child see me.

Be quiet. Children are stronger than you think. I wasn't so sure but being even less certain about whom I was talking to, decided to keep quiet and let my memories spread around me.

It is important, I decided, to let your memories 'land'. Like an aeroplane. I knew about aeroplanes and how you could hold its nose up and float along the runway, just inches above it, until the thing gasped "Enough! Put me down please. *Let me land.*" And that moment, once landed, is when the nostalgia kicks in. Why think about the day my wonderful school burned down when there were so many more, earlier, beautiful memories of such a wonderful place? Why not float a while, inches above it all and then, and only then, slowly put it down among the rubble? In the smoke where you can't quite see the solid ground beneath but you know it's firm enough. Threading through charred timbers, crunching them to dust, until coming to rest within a clear space. Beside lines of school kids, passing precious books from one to another, out towards an increasing pile in distant safety on some other green slope.

Even there you could see a wisp of smoke lazily rising.

They cancelled my Latin exam due at 9am that Friday morning. They mentioned that in the newspaper although they didn't give my name. But it was still the first time anyone seemed to remember me.

No, instead we go charging in at top speed, 'flapless to land' as they would call it, and groove our way regardless through years of memories and mystery - sadly disrespectful of all who had gone before and who had added their own timbers and bricks to the various walls. Except all the timbers had gone and there were no bricks where we lived. The school was built of granite blocks. Which was why the burned-out building, everything inside made of wood destroyed, stood grimly and permanently, with silent, dwindling drifts of smoke circling upwards in its own final epitaph to those who had gone before.

Years later, they offered me a guided tour of the new building whenever I should pass that way. (I had in fact paid one earlier visit but more of that later. No, we'll forget that one ... I took the lady who died there and will close that chapter with her visit). But how could I tour it again now, I thought, looking down at my crippled limbs (... which is another reason why we'll forget it). It's a bit embarrassing having to explain. I wasn't sure about the words 'cripple' or 'spastic' until a medic confirmed their validity for me. Dysfunctional, he said, it means that something cannot function any more, it's alright to use it. We use it still, he said. Crippled. Spastic. It's alright to use those words. So, I quietened my aversion to everything associated with them. Medics told me, we use them still. But I can tell you that it's not alright being a cripple or being a spastic.

No! I shouted at the retreating medics. No, I wept in my next authentic display of emotion. Validity, authenticity, I thought sniffily as only a screwed up social scientist can. There's a difference – cripple that when you pocket your next pay cheque. *Spastic that!*

Suddenly, I had turned quite nasty. I was spitting resentment and aiming wildly at nothing in particular – and with whatever came to hand. At anyone. Needlessly. The medics were wonderful but they just happened to be in the way. So, I concluded as any academic puzzles these things out, nostalgia starts with wonder, then changes into pain and finally contaminates whatever is within reach.

But in truth, it only contaminates the self. The self or the soul? The self – it's safer.

Pleased with myself for having achieved at least a swirling alliteration (I briefly thought of Dervishes, did they swirl?), my thoughts returned to the dinner tray and the spoon, the knife and the fork upon it …

No, came an interruption from the corner, *Dervishes whirl and spin and they are something of a nuisance and a distraction.* You don't want to know about them.

Relieved that nothing on my dinner tray was doing any of that at that moment, I again picked the implements up in turn. I discovered very quickly that I could not manage the fork in my left hand, in the way I had always used it. Anything in my right hand was safe.

Sorry let me rephrase that:

"Anyone in the vicinity of my right hand, whenever it was holding anything sharp, was *probably* safe."

You can imagine the risks in being close to the left: worse the risks of being close to the right if ever a red mist descended. As I write, a play is on the radio … the radio ... I am sorry, I fell asleep and now I have forgotten again. That's what happens when you take buckets of pills like I do. Oh-ho, self-pity.

I've found some pills down the side of my seat cushion, where you dropped them, said the wheelchair in a gentle tone of voice. You fell asleep but don't worry, that's what I am here for, to help you. I found them.

That was the kindest thing I had heard for many a day and I expressed my very grateful thanks to my wheelchair. And with that, we both went finally to sleep.

I turned my attention to the question of place. My method, I recalled was to triangulate –

Good grief, I heard from the corner, there ain't nothing triangular over 'ere, it's round, all round. ('Wheels,' it added in case I hadn't understood.)

'All round' echoed for several minutes between the various corners of my rectangular room in a haze of trigonometry. My mind began to close down in a geometric muddle but still would not leave the problem of place alone. If I could pin down one particular place, I could then see how actions and words intersected there. There! Yes, there! That's where I come from, would be the result.

Now you're making sense, biy, now you're making sense.

And so, I began at the beginning and worked my way through. Well, that was the plan anyway.

When we got bored staring at the empty page, the wheelchair took me for a wander through the *Re*-hab hospital, its point being, I suppose, that place-present is far more meaningful than place-past. I began to reflect upon someone who might be obsessed, or at least greatly pre-occupied, with a place in his or her past. And I could not come to any clearer image than an amalgam of Winston Churchill and the Hunchback of *Notre Dame*. At this point I was showered with oaths and curses from the wheelchair whose education had clearly not extended to either British history or French romantic drama. The result, the 'showering of oaths and curses', was rather like being flailed, I *imagine*. Like being subjected to endless transmissions of the

Simpsons. At least, that was the conclusion I came to as we trundled along the corridor under the main spar of the aircraft. I could not protest. I could only submit. Eventually the flailing stopped. Whether the Simpsons continues to be broadcast, I have never bothered to find out.

By the time we had reached the end of the main spar – *corridor*, came the anticipated correction – it had dawned upon me that without new stimulus, it was very difficult to think deeply of another location when pre-occupied with where you are at present. That may be a function of stroke, of having to concentrate, for example, on not falling over. It is, boy, muttered the wheelchair unpleasantly, it is: I can tell you that I would far rather be somewhere else, *an-bhfuil tú ag teacht liom*? No, I wasn't really *with* him as the question demanded, I was *in* him. And so we trundled silently back again. The left foot plate had long since fallen off: I was carrying it. The wheelchair kept reminding me that if he didn't concentrate on where we were going, we would both end up on the floor.

On my desk at home, I remembered by way of distraction, diversion and distance from place-present, was a beautiful carved wooden head. Made of teak. Life-sized. Very heavy. It was a life-sized 'Bali head', I recalled, because the graceful style and gentle features were those of the Island of Bali. My own poor head felt as solid and heavy as the Bali head but without any of its beauty. My mother had bought the head in Singapore just after the War in Asia had finished. Something perfect to emerge from a wholly wretched, awful, terrible experience.

"Percival, that fecker Percival," mouthed the wheelchair, recalling the one-time leader of the Auxiliaries and the Black and Tans who, two decades later, had surrendered Singapore – the one thing army-Brits were baptised at birth not to do. Of such details, painful then delicious, are Irish memories made (except, as you'll learn, in my case the memory had a sting in the tail).

"Well, I know where you come from," I replied reflecting that the wheelchair's knowledge of history was not as bad as all that. Anyway, back to the Bali Head.

I bought it in Teng's Emporium on River Valley Road, she would tell me. And then, about six weeks before my stroke, my wife and I had some Chinese visitors to dinner, parents and their very bright, urbane and international daughter. They lived in Singapore but were ethnically but not politically Chinese, just some-time, one-time emigrants from Shanghai. My mother bought it in Singapore at … , I began to trot out the old story, faltering when it occurred to me that our guests might themselves have painful family memories. But they seemed not to. So, … Teng's in River Valley Road, I finished.

There followed some Chinese cooing and clucking as the parents poured over the Bali head until the father said that no, they did not know of any Teng's in Singapore. But we do live in River Valley Road, interjected the bored daughter who had noticed the greater truth to have eluded her parents. It taught me something about place – What? asked the wheelchair annoyingly. That some things are easily forgettable, I hissed through my clenched teeth.

In fact, the truth was rather simpler. Our Chinese visitors routinely thought of River Valley Road in Chinese: it was their mother-tongue. The daughter, in contrast, was multilingual with English probably dominant. Not unnaturally, the place-present of the Bali Head upon our kitchen table was more intelligible to them in Chinese than the place-past of River Valley Road was in English.

Wot did yer 'ave to eat? asked the wheelchair who was sounding decidedly Cockney. Eels? Did yer 'ave eels? I loves eels … (and then tearfully) … I aven't 'ad 'em fer ages.

I ignored its lack of appreciation, its vulgarity and its generally low tact, sensitivity and taste. And I definitely ignored the tears which were definitely reptilian in origin. At that moment, everything about the wheelchair revolted me. Say nothing, I thought. And so I thought and remembered nothing, too, not even the handfuls of eels hanging from the bushes along the Tail Race on the Shannon after a heavy discharge from Ardnacrusha power station. Who said eels were a Cockney relish? Oi did, oi did, I could hear echoing somewhere.

Realising that my beautiful Bali Head might be leading me somewhere, I returned to the root causes of forgettability and memorability – of security, mood, pain, happiness, companions … The ideas kept flooding in. I realised I had taken the first step down the ladder of abstraction and that it was just a matter of putting these ideas all in order. I waited for some oath or smart remark from the corner where it had been pushed but, surprisingly, there was none.

"Are you alright over there?" I asked.

"Fine,"it answered. "I just don't do ladders … "

I smirked, pleased at having won one over.

" … and neither do you at the moment, I notice," continued the voice smugly.

I took four case studies, these being the places I thought that might include the elusive starting point. Well, one of them certainly did but, I realised, it was immediately dismissible for producing insufficient hits against my ordered ideas. And this alarmed me because it was all too easy: the first was easy to exclude and then the other three came tumbling down. And returning later to this point, I find once again that I have forgotten them all. Oh dear. Perhaps
I had made a mistake with my methodology –

" – *method*, boy, not methodology. They are different things," interrupted my tutor with the wheels on. Not for the first time, I took the point but still ignored him and pressed on. No, the method was sound despite the human being's annoying preference for living in the present. There was just some other problem I had yet to isolate. Nothing over 'ere to be isolated, came a persistent thought. Nothing over 'ere.

Where then? I wondered, where then? And so I went back and back until there was nowhere else to think about.

His mother had described for him the ways of prison camps in the time of the war in Asia and instilled in him the inmates' acceptance that fate ruled their lives. But fate was an individual event with an equally distinguishable potential for discontinuity and disruption.

Oh God, 'ere we go again.

More often, fate could bring inner peace and calm if totally submitted to. And submit they did, each of them in their own ways and as far as they felt able, in order to survive. Of course, some did not manage that act of absolute trust and committal but, being women confined together, found the reward of even a partial 'act of faith' generally more attainable than male prisoners might.

Male prisoners. Men. Mates.

Protection – out of reach and emasculated, too. Dangerous even for their situation.

The men were over there, upon the hillside on the other slope of that baleful stretch of jungle, but I did not come from there. The women found it easier, after a while, to keep their heads down and not to look beyond the wire, and would have said something different. Only the weekly visits of the priest, intended to bring peace, reliably left them in turmoil for the whispered messages he would confuse and half-forget on the gruelling, filthy, mosquito-blown path between the camps. And then there were the blows of the guards to contend with, too. On such an abysmal diet, in such an awful climate and cowed by such physical maltreatment, how could the poor man have managed to survive all that and still make sense of anything they urgently told him to pass on? *Does anyone recognise this scrap of hand-writing?* Or to take back. *I can tell you that your husband is alive.*

By submitting to fate, decisions were taken somewhere else – by the flutter of butterfly wings that might ease, if not even take completely away, the burdens of their cruel existence. It was such a twist of fate that brought the women together in the early days of their internment. The need of each, to be held and soothed, was overriding and my young mother took some young girl into her arms where they both wept their grief and pain out into the sun-baked dust until their hair had almost completely tangled and turned them into one, calmer, mutual sense of possible continued existence. And perhaps, in spite of the dirt and deprivation, even survival, too, and an eventual return to normality. That became their initial reason for living and probably tempered her ultimate approach to me.

The shared experience, of passage from devastation into hope, laid the foundation for a relationship that would endure. Soon, their secrets would be exchanged, while all the time I grew inside my mother's womb. Other women, older women, kindly souls with enormous experience – but not, of course, experience of a hell-hole such as this – helped them all on the way. And, with the mysteries of new life and of nurturing existence on the extreme margins, a new baby would become their dominant will to continue in the task of living and surviving.

They would come through it and I would, too, but not quite as one of them.

Somewhere on that journey, she acquired the Bali head – a gesture perhaps, to me, which I still dutifully loved although I could not have come from there. Not anywhere from there.

All I could say about it was: that was the point at which I realised how I, by and large, preferred things to people. Not only do I still have my Bali Head on the desk-top in front of me. But I also have my Teddy Bear on one of the bookshelves behind me. Teddy came from Colombo and is about a year or two older than me. And he is certainly fitter than me, too. There are many other things as well but I won't go into them.

The bungalow was set back from the beach – a typical beach in the Indian Ocean with wind sweeping in from the sea and tall palm trees, appearing to lean against it like improbable one-legged ostriches. Where the trees grew thickly further along the beach, they looked shorter and more upright, a feather-fringed flock crowded together listening to the conversations along the sands. The bungalow itself had a tiled terrace or veranda running around the entire walls with a shady overhang and pillars along its length. Shutters were open by day and closed by night across each floor-to-ceiling window. And uniform criss-cross railings, with a hand-rail along the top, joined each pillar to the next in a gesture to Dutch colonial tastes. The garden was cleared and open except for fine-leaved trees each casting scarce but much needed shade. Where chairs and tables were placed, they were all within that shade or along the veranda, and all designed for relaxing, for conversation, for feet up and for enjoying the passage of time. And all the time, the sun came and went, structuring the passing of the day and the socialising of the evening.

They had a photograph somewhere of his mother, recovering slowly from her war-time experiences and standing with her first domestic staff.

'Staff'. What colonial arrogance, muttered the wheelchair who was suddenly sounding very thoughtful and educated. I am a republican, he continued. It was my turn to lift my eyes to the heavens: who could imagine that politics could be so pervasive? My type hid revolvers, you know, came an angry thought circling round me like a wasp. And when you think about it, boy, it snarled, the British Auxiliaries destroyed everything and the act of destruction, being political, anointed even the rubble with a political nobility. I gasped quietly that the wheelchair could think and articulate like that, and then responded. But clearing the rubble away and then the act of reconstruction removed that aura ... which makes you just a wheelchair.

We didn't speak for a long time after that which taught me several lessons. First, by way of reinforcement, that even the inanimate can extend a form of friendship – companionship through the hard times when broken minds rage and fume at their inabilities. Second, even inanimate objects can help define the new possibilities after something so damaging and destructive as a stroke. After all, apart from your memories, the inanimate is all you've then got to work with. And third, the sudden cessation of contact with familiar, supportive things is initially a backward step in the process of recovery. I thought of my Bali Head, the only thing that remained (and Teddy), and how things would be without it. But it does open up new possibilities. Superman, I thought. No, came a voice disappearing out of the haze, super-wheelchair …

My thoughts returned to the photograph. It concealed an affable, well-oiled domestic organisation – a colonially reproduced arrangement within the house, within each house. The truth in that part of the world was that those in sore distress would make petitions, that decisions would be made, that measures would need to be provided and that charity would be dispersed. There was nothing hidden, it was all on the surface. In this way, the world worked on and stability was retained. Each household budget, for example, was feeding more than the people who worked inside the house and that at least one family beyond the compound, where the jungle grew more thickly, was also being supported on the incomes within. It was understood and accepted. Interesting and half-remembered but he didn't come from there.

On the left in the photograph was a man wearing a white tunic and loose trousers, and on his mother's right was a man with an identical tunic but underneath it a man's sarong. Both wore loose, leather slippers. Each had thick, lustrous hair brushed back so that their high foreheads were revealed and sun-catching. His mother wore a cotton dress with open neck and short sleeves. A narrow belt around her waist emphasised how slight she was herself and how much weight she had lost.

When they brought him home from hospital, a baby weak by the misfortune of camp-birth, Cookie (latter-day colonials loved endearments like that), who was not in the photograph, stood inside the front door with his hands outstretched. Love of children, especially the master's children, even more their own, was typical of the people there. Everything was so steady, so predictable and so reliable in that world, he thought. But there was no response from the wheelchair, which he regretted.

Untypically, however, his father handed the baby to this senior member of his household. The man was delighted and cooed in native tongue to the small child while his father walked on inside and his mother similarly detached herself from this modest little home-coming. Cookie took the baby to show the others and then along the veranda to a small room which had been specially prepared. Inside was a cot covered in a large white linen cloth and a table similarly draped.

With a flourish, one of the houseboys, the one wearing the sarong in the photograph, pulled the two linen cloths away. And scattered along the little mattress of the cot, and among the neatly folded nappies, creams and cotton wool, were drifts of orange marigold petals, freshly gathered outside. Marigold petals brought honour to the new arrival. If his parents seemed less than enthusiastic about the new arrival, the household was wild with joy and did not mind in the slightest that the whole had to be scrubbed and sanitised all over again. Soon, the marigolds and sunlight brought strength to his tiny limbs

Accepted and welcomed in this way, he might have come from there but for the first of two unconnected incidents.

His parents had gone up-country. The weather was uncomfortably hot. It was a good reason for them to escape to the hills. Up there, the climate was wonderfully cool and fresh in comparison. Their intention was from there to go on to Kandy and then to the heights of Nuwara Eliyah on the way back.

It's actually pronounced 'new raylia', he remembered – and then recalled a spiteful little Benedictine monk back in Ireland who tried to trap him five decades later by deliberately mispronouncing the name of the nearby landscaped garden of Sigiriya. 'Sigoria' he called it, with a glint in his eye, rather than Sig-i-ria. But I got him, I remembered, by correcting him in Irish: *níl, ní mar sin ...*

While they were away, the household routine relaxed. Nanny brought her friends round for tea in the garden and their respective charges came too. And hospitality was next returned between them. On one of these occasions, a dog found its way through the outer compound and into the garden in question. And nobody noticed. He loved dogs but nobody noticed.

Rabid dogs, or pi-dogs as they were called, don't behave like healthy dogs. They don't stand up properly. They lollop and lean to one side. As if they too have had a stroke, he mused. They look immediately suspicious. (Do I look immediately suspicious, he wondered. Is that why nobody comes to talk to me?) Yet nobody noticed this slavering, lethal monster who was working its way closer and closer to the crawling babies. And then, of them all, it licked *him*. And next it bit him.

The child screamed but the cries of the assembled nannies rose louder still. The houseboys came running and the dog was beaten off. The police were called and someone shot it. They all heard the explosion. The child was rushed to the local hospital while an urgent message was sent to his parents far away in the hills.

The treatment for rabies was and remains horrific, he explained to the silent wheelchair. It is a truly appalling prospect for an adult bitten by a rabid dog … but for a baby? I won't go into the detail but I was very, very lucky indeed to survive the experience and to come through the series of appalling injections that have to be administered. Administered in the stomach, incidentally … and just think how tiny a baby's stomach is.

Crucially, however, the whole business seems to have thrown a switch in his mother's mind if the switch had not already been firmly deselected. Perhaps she had been so deeply shocked by what she had already experienced that this latest baby was somehow less fortunate, less deserving of attention, than others she had vested her emotions in. Perhaps it was even jealousy that her own child now suffered far greater attention than she ever did herself. Here, he recalled her related childhood memories of abusing a cat by tying it in her pram and wheeling it, mewing piteously, around the neighbourhood. And what she did to her own teddy bear, up the old washing pole in the garden, just doesn't bear mentioning.

"What has he done today?" inquired an elderly neighbour hoisting her own washing up a nearby pole, suggesting that my mother was habitually cruel or at least indifferent – and that the neighbourhood had noticed.

The second incident was far more straightforward. His father's tour of duty was over and the family was called home. Except it wasn't his home and never could be. England under rationing. England full of bomb-sites and ruined buildings. England with places where he could go provided he wrapped up well and didn't pick up anything.

England? He doesn't like it here, he would hear his mother saying frequently over the remaining years of his childhood and teens. Quite right, he thought. Quite right. I never liked it there. Here. I do not want to be here. Why did you not leave me there?

And as for that other place they were leaving. Well, it was soon gone and with it the noise and colour and delicious scents of the Far East. I'll always remember, mused his mother to herself looking back at an empty horizon, I could smell the scents before I could see the place. All he could smell was the sea, fuel oil and ship's furnaces as they ploughed their way west and north, with his young memories ditched, useless and floating in the wake where they would finally sink and disappear.

It seems clear that detachment and diversion were decided at that point. He was cast, not adrift, but at the end of a tow rope in the aptly named Doldrums. Dependent and doldrummed. But in the way that life can really twist its screws, the whole damn delicious thing would soon be repeated.

I have an image in my mind of an adult man dancing gently with a young girl, presumably his daughter, in his arms. It is my impression that when adults dance together, their visual field varies from sequence to sequence. In one, the man at least will be concerned with navigation and collision avoidance. Next, he might shift his view to his partner's face where he will look her in the eyes or, fleetingly, at some feature of her face, hair etc. She in return will be doing something similar although one imagines that a woman's optimal field of vision will include more colours, clothes and contrasts than the man will have observed. Anyway, that's what they are looking at, and why, in my opinion. What they are looking at changes frequently; you can see the field of vision alter almost with every bar and beat. Their thoughts are mostly elsewhere.

The man holding his daughter is not much different but she is. He is lost in the middle to far distance, while she is looking unblinkingly at some feature of her beloved father. To call it staring is wrong. She is looking, with open unblinking eyes and very close to what she wants to see. Her eyes may be just an inch or two from the side of his head, or some other feature, but it is more than the proximity that captures our attention: it is her open eyes, their focal point somewhere within his skull. Sat in my chair, I can sense her looking deep inside him. Something I do not think a boy would do, to either his mother or his father.

This daughter-to-father bond is a curious, lovely thing to see, a total, 100% preoccupation with the first man in her life.

So why does it not seem to happen in adult years? Where and when did it disappear? Was it just a candid display of childhood, unquestioning love or something more complex – perhaps a visual fascination for one or more features of parental power? Baby boys, I imagine, would show something similar in their eyes and faces during feeding, but probably not later. I do not know the answer. But, equally, I do not recall seeing that same unblinking gaze in a young male at all. I may have had it once, I think, and when I was older, say about 12 years old, but she destroyed it quickly, unthinkingly, uncaringly and permanently. When some later tour of paternal duty was over, I had been sent down from Scotland on the train, in my kilt and tweed jacket, to join my father in south west England. I managed the journey, with five changes (Stirling, Glasgow, Manchester,

Birmingham and Bristol), by myself. Not bad, I thought and still think. My mother stayed behind – to clear things up. About 2 months later, 'things' had been sufficiently cleared up for our little family to be reunited. We met on a dirty railway platform in Manchester where something trivial went dreadfully wrong and maternal anger quickly spilled over, destroying the planned, peaceful reunion and slashing away at the reins. Enough said: it was a turning point. No, a point of departure.

My father achieved some similar familial detachment and completed the job when, at about the same age, he struck me down. Physically. But this was the same man whose hand I had later held for hours and hours in dementia-land, a son-to-father gesture of love and concern that just could not quite compare with the dizzy-twisted images of a young girl dancing with her Dad. At best,

I seemed a lightning rod for things he and I had done together. Is that what he thought, I wondered as I stared at him, lying mountainous on his air-pumped bed with all its paraphernalia around. Where is dementia-land? And is he happy there?

I sensed a slight squeeze. And yet I recalled far more on the day my mother and I sat either side of him watching a couple ballroom dance for the care patients' entertainment and stimulation. My poor old Dad was furious with us both. I don't know how I knew or at what point I realised the truth about his mood for he didn't move a muscle and could not anyway speak. Suffice it to say, he was furious; I knew it but she didn't. I could never enter his dementia-world and even when presented to his young man's-world, a younger boy myself taken on a visit, I never entered his world. I merely captured curious, disconnected images which confirmed for me that I could recognise him doing something unremarkable – in my mind's eye, I can *see* him doing this or that and in this place. And there is my grandfather, over there doing something equally unremarkable in a garden plot. Is that my grandfather? Yes, they replied, go over to see him. And that is what I did for, in those days, children did as they were told. I always, nearly always, did as I was told for fear of that threat: … *or I will tell your father when he gets home.*

Ours was not an uncaring home. I was very fortunate and remain grateful but I am still acutely aware of things that, if done differently, could have changed my life beyond all recognition. My young life was run on guilt and administered with fear and nothing changed but passing decades. Small wonder Zarathustra climbed his mountain. And small wonder, I continued out loud, that no-one since could or would follow me through the foothills.

Small wonder, I shouted, that I could only mark my progress by super-things like snakes, nannies that other people never experienced and a wonder-full wheelchair that spoke and thought and theorised.

I listened. Oh how I listened but no answer came. It was as lonely being perfect, I decided, as the other way around. But how could I even imagine the space that lay in between and ask could I ever have come from the hillsides down there?

Seeking ecstasy, or at least release, for neither of which they could produce a drug that worked for me, I stepped quickly and lightly across the hilltops of my personal history wherever sunlight still fell. There were not many such places and often, too often it seemed, I had to jump. It became like a game – leaping across the Burnsides, jumping over pi-dogs – until I found a camp on one hill and a ditch on another where people in striped rags lay clustered waiting for my attention. How could I have clear, coherent images of one geographical end of the Second World Atrocity and yet also from the other?

Because that was all she would tell you about, came the voice which was not that of the wheelchair. The voice was right: she even called me in from fishing in the burn outside to tell me that someone was coming to tea who had been captured behind enemy lines and … and dealt with as the spy he was. Why tell a child a thing like that? After the visit perhaps but not beforehand.

Because she was living and re-living it herself.

They all were. For them, it all remained current and very vivid. And she wanted you to share it. She was desperate for you to share it.

Yes, it still made it very obvious to me that no-one would follow me through the foothills.

For I was different: I came from my mother's memories and nowhere else. Perhaps I inherited her memories. Perhaps she needed to pass them on, a generational burden she could no longer carry alone. Her personal cross. And perhaps their social circle noticed and, like osmosis, the information filtered down. What information? Where did it filter down? Her brother, my uncle, was torpedoed three times and survived. She herself ran and dived over a wall as a land mine floated down only yards the other side. The explosion was deafening, she said. Why couldn't she say it was terrifying, that she screamed and wept? *Because what came next was worse.*

Her tale was of grim and unrelenting destruction and loss. It was teeth-gritting, brave and endlessly … endlessly … oh, contrived and unreal. Perhaps she felt the need to catch up? Once she said, for example, as she shook me by the shoulders, we were fighting for our lives

– fighting for our lives! And then I had to do it all again. Don't you understand? God, I felt I had to fight for my own life – once, twice, three times even – for there was nothing gently osmotic about her grip. And later, only later, did I understand where some of her fervour might elsewhere have derived from: a whole new dimension to 'fighting for our lives'.

My Grand-uncle had half his hand shot away by snipers in the First World Atrocity. My Grand-father was a Colour Sergeant in Gallipoli, the Dardanelles and the Somme.

Do you know what that means? she would cry as my immature unknowing mind would wrestle with what a trench might be and always being the first 'over the top' to face death by gunfire: hearing the bullets but not knowing where the target was. Wondering about Irishmen pretending allegiance for the honour of being shot, or not. How did my Grand-father survive? Do you know that his legacy to me was the information that the Turkish snipers were like crows in the trees – and that came via her.

Why did they never tell me when he died many years later in his bed? In solemn fact, they never told me when any of them died. Were they shutting out him, them, or their memories in? And whatever the answer, what did that do for me? What did it say about their regard or respect for me? Why did such hidden memories only emerge when stuffed with a pill that would lift my mood? A pill that was administered by a third party medic, unknowingly, in a another country? And, more importantly, what would be in the space left behind in me when the effect of the drug wore off?

Impermanence, I decided. And that was being kind. Vulnerability. But was it not also despair? Or simply devastating loneliness? Something not even my own baby daughter ever chose to stare inside and investigate? I recall that Nietzsche called this void 'a celestial naught'[4]: the space left behind when

---

[4] Nietzsche, *Also Sprach Zarathustra*

the effect of the drugs wore off. Nothing. Heavenly nothing.

When would it ever stop, I wondered. Stop sufficient to allow me to build my own memories. Or had I become so perishable, so frail and brittle, that with the slightest change of temperature I would evaporate like the snows of yesteryear, or disappear like smoke in the wind?

That would be very appropriate, I thought, for then I would join my Grandfather. But unfortunately, my family doesn't do cemeteries and I wouldn't know where to look for him or indeed any of them. Only when the drugs cut in did I discover that it was possible to step out of melancholy and self-pity, and healthily recall good thoughts of the past – except that the mood-lifters didn't stop there. They were an essential part of my retrospective cocktail: they provided the landscape within which I could distinguish dark foothills from patches of light[5]. And yet they forced upon me troublesome, parallel conversations with myself. This was the price of the better effects, I decided. But who was responsible and who cared anyway?

I began to develop the theory that conditioning a child with the experiences of previous generations while preventing them from gaining any foothold of their own produced the consequence that the child would seek to exceed, to outdo, the impact of the previous generations – but be destined to fail like an *Untermensch*[6] in the attempt. *Untermenschlich* seemed like my mother, as

---

[5] *Ibid.*, from *VII. Reading and Writing*.
[6] The word *Untermensch* means 'sub-human' but is better known as a dreadful, dreadful Nazi label for any poor shred of human existence that did not match the Nazi's sick criteria for being Arian.

well as me. She had a bloody great chip on her shoulder which turned her, by way of self-defence, into an enduring snob. Such children were never grounded. They could only float in the semi-dark, fed with pills and family history, involuntary cowards when faced with reality, morality being an ephemeral thing –

Oh no, biy, came a surprising interjection.

Where have you been, I asked, but no explanation for the wheelchair's absence was forthcoming.

You've got it mostly right but now you're at risk.

Of what, I asked.

Of going off the rails, it continued. Anyway, I'm back and you had better sharpen up. Oh God, I prayed, please protect me from all things round – from little pills to big wheelchairs. I shut my eyes tightly and lay to attention in my bed but could only think of sharp things like needles, things associated with hospitals, things that hurt.

It seemed that the wheelchair did not like the idea of morality being ephemeral. Morality, I thought. Are you talking doctrine, like ethics? I asked. Or are you talking qualities that make you right or wrong? Or practices, like collectively hearing opinions and weighing their impact? (It was my turn, I decided, to be the picking little pain in the arse.)

I listened very carefully but the damn thing seemed to be fast asleep. But I still managed to put my finger on the answer. It was troubling: morality was power. Or, more precisely, power determined morality. And that was relativistic. Power could only be ephemeral, too. In my experience, I realised, morality had no intrinsic authority, it did not convey a right to power, although that might appear to be the case. I thought of the black soutanes walking, talking and organising. What happened, I wondered, when they took those funny tunics off? And only many years later did I realise the awful truth for some young, tragic unfortunates, that such power did not need any clothes when enforcing local immoral truths.

Oh dear, I was getting confused. In hospital, as in recovery, it is possible to find much welcome diversion in constant television where the category 'documentaries' can expose the broken mind to the half-remembered, human tragedies of the twentieth century which it has no need to tangle with. And yet there is a market for it and the spiral of truth and counter-truth continues unabatedly and unsatisfactorily. A Nazi soldier had no power when stripped of his uniform and might even find himself shipped off, cattle-wagoned off in a case of mis-identification … But then my thoughts shuddered to a halt. My mind could just not distinguish between a naked priest and a naked Nazi and subsequent questions about morality fell mercifully and unaddressed into the dismal, desperate dirt around their feet.

I don't like the direction this is taking, commented my wheelchair. Help me please, I answered. Concentrate on power, it replied, not the abuses in our history books, not the narrative you were subjected to, or the contradictions thrown up by relativism and objectivism.

He was right. There were enough broken people in society without my arriving unwanted on one or other of their tragic stockpiles. But where did this wheelchair come from? How did he learn to think and speak like this, to understand, apparently, the difference between challenging philosophical concepts?

The Garridge, came the answer which I interpreted as 'garage'. The Wheelchair Shed, where else? Good Gawd.

I was stunned at realising that wheelchairs enjoyed a sort of depot for weekly chats and reminiscences, like Mens' Sheds. I decided instead that, like walls, wheelchairs could somehow absorb the thoughts and conversation of their various cargos.

Have you carried many well-known personalities? I asked.

None, he said, and I don't see much changing round 'ere for a while. Oh dear. That was a bit deflating but I persevered: what do you talk about in the gar … in the Garridge? I asked. We plug ourselves in for rest, recuperation, repair and a top-up, was the reply.

What do you mean by 'top-up'? I asked again.

We believe that the soul is separate from the body, it continued in a superior tone of voice, and therefore that much can be learned from just listening. We share what we have heard.

Wow! I responded, and then: how long are you going to be around?

That depends on you. When it comes to the 'orspital, we 'old only one objective moral truth, that people in 'orspital shall 'ave their own wheelchair.

It took me a while to work that one out. How do you get better without wanting to be discharged? Do they ever sell off used ones, I asked tentatively. Used whats, came the reply.

Wheelchairs, I said, wheelchairs.

Silence. Nada. Nothing.

That's disappointing. I wanted to know what else he believed in.

As the weeks passed, I discovered that there was a difference between silence and nothing. Silence is a wilful thing. Not answering. Shutting out the world so that distraction cannot disturb. Nothing is being in a void. Tumbling. Helpless. Like being stuffed in the corner of my sub-ward's private toilet, held up, fenced in, to prevent my falling over by a convenient extension from a piece of ward equipment. All I did was to ring the bell to go to the loo, the second time in one hour to the annoyance of the overworked night nurse. And so she stuffed me up in the corner as someone else's bedside bell began to toll incessantly through the dimly lit corridor. She was Mediterranean, the inward-recruited night nurse, and had wonderful flashing eyes as well as a huge sense of humour. She stuffed me up, so she did, as the other bell began to ring more urgently still. You move, she hissed, *and I kill you.* Her eyes shone like two wide slits. I believed her, crossed my legs and held my breath until she got back.

As I said, there is a difference between silence and nothing. I did nothing and I said nothing until she returned. And just for the record, I still thought she was a first-class nurse. But as a long-term inmate in hospital, I noted also that silence and nothing could easily begin to merge if you submitted to the optimal ward culture of neatness, order and a general sense of calm and cleanliness. My advice? Get into bed and stay there. They'll wake you up for the next meal. Until then play dead: no-one will trouble you unless they really have to. Just leave one arm out so that they can easily take your blood pressure. Play half-dead and even the medical students and their task books will soon fade quietly away. The only distraction came when the wheelchair whistled quietly in my ear. Wake up, boy, you're wanted. And then, decanted from the bed and secured in the wheelchair, the pair of us would be whisked away again, sometimes talking, sometimes not. He stopped me being lazy and would generally ask me topical questions, just to keep me on the right side of nothing

The same sense of precarious balance between silence and nothing occurred at home, once discharged, except that the wheelchair couldn't accompany me. I won't go into our parting which I found more distressing than he did. In fact he started rolling away before I had got out and into the car.

"Look out!" they cried.

"Don't worry," I replied, "he's only doing it on purpose. He won't let anything happen." And, as I had predicted, he didn't. And the moment passed without anyone remembering although I did. It was a bit like growing out of your first real bike and having to walk away and leave it. Except that old bikes don't communicate and wheelchairs always start to move first. In fact, they never go away until they are ready to discharge you.

When I got home, I discovered to my delight that they had left my Bali Head upon my desk. *Om Swastiastu*, I intoned, as I offered my Head the Sembah[7]. Did the finely

---

[7] The Sembah is the Balinese version of the familiar, Eastern nod of the head with both hands held palms together, fingers pointing upwards. 'Om Swastiatsu' is the traditional, Balinese greeting accompanying the Sembah.

carved eyelids move, I wondered. They certainly did once I had swallowed the next bucket of pills. But then I soon found myself whirled round and back to the days of the camps. Oh dear.

I felt close enough but I still knew that I didn't come from there.

It became easier, therefore, to 'coast' between silence and nothing. To keep a very low profile, to sleep even, because it was easier for household management for me just to 'coast'. It was also a more effective way of keeping the dizziness under control – just lying immobile on the bed. This also helped the swelling legs and made certain exercises easier. But the truth was that I put on weight. I got fat. (Someone told me that the pills have that effect. Personally, I thought it was more probably the chocolate I was smuggling in.) And when I was called back for an

Outpatient's appointment, you-know-who was waiting there and soon began cursing the extra payload. It continued that way, every time I returned for an appointment and yet I appreciated the sense of continuity.

That wheelchair and I were a team. At least, that's what I thought. And that's what drugs can do to you, along with all the other curious impressions and hallucinations. They cocoon you in such a void that your world is marked by inanimate, nonsensical relationships and questionable conversations. As Huxley observed, citing a philosopher called Dr C. D. Broad, the brain and nervous system, being protective rather than productive, are there to sift out the irrelevant and nonsensical. And if mine were both damaged, small wonder that my world was marked in such a way.

Perhaps the medication creates such intolerable pressures upon whatever remains of your mind and memory that your own need for companionship stimulates these relationships. That, to me, makes sense. I can understand it. But what about people like me who believe they have no need of companionship? I am comfortable with my Bali Head – and until discharged was comfortable with the prospect, *maximam partem*, of being reunited. Why did I end up without asking for it with a wheelchair from the richer, more educated end of the Garridge?

The days passed without change, like cards being dealt endlessly with no deviation. My study had become my bedroom. Our sitting room had become my study. I still studied, sat and slept there but the places I did them each in changed. I imposed a small degree of change upon myself if only to alter my awareness of this circular relationship. My Bali Head gazed only upon the writing pad in front of me but I could swivel and raise my field of view to target different bookshelves and artefacts. And that brought a welcome release. I discovered that I could test my recollection of the narratives held within, that I did not need to climb or clamber just to reach a particular volume (I couldn't do either anyway). And that induced me, in turn, to think carefully about a particular historical thread – after all, history was all I had to play with. I could do very little for myself that was original or refreshingly new: I could only repeat the daily routines the physiotherapists had approved while my mind took flights of fancy.

What's new, came an unexpected interruption.

Where   are
you, I spoke out
loud.

Flying fancy, like you.

Good grief, I pondered, there seems to be no getting away from him. His permanent proximity destines me, so I thought, to 'down'. I am dependent upon his reactions when the best advice available is 'up' – fasten your gaze upon the horizon. Do *not* look down for fear that you will topple. Do *not* look back, go forward.

And that's what I think, too, governor, offered the wheelchair. Don't misunderstand me. I am here to help not to hinder. You set the destination and what we shall do en route, and I'll 'old yer 'and. We'll get yah froo' dis stroke togevver.

I quite liked the cockney in him. Even when it was nearly unintelligible. It made his undeniable vulgarity just about acceptable. So, cut out the self-pity is what he was telling me, just get on with it.

And that is what we then did next.

The first thing we planned to do was to trip back through the foothills, not to refresh or replenish my memory, but to identify every single thing that helped to make Me on the journey so far. Let me repeat the important bit which I think could be easily lost: … that helped to make and fabricate and manufacture and mould *me* on the journey so far.

I can think of none in my acquaintance who undertook this task, for two reasons. And this is the gift I offer you, friend, if you have laboured and struggled this far.

First, it is normal, the general experience, that families identify with one particular place. Successive generations born and brought up in that place each suffer for the sake of it. And that is how they, how each one makes his or her mark – they suffer a little bit more than their predecessors. How they suffer is important. As I said, they suffer for the sake of it: they find some new quality or feature. They are like rock-climbers searching with urgent finger tips for some new fissure, crack or crevice – for a new route up the increasingly difficult wall. And once you can hang from what you and you alone have discovered, a new energy is released and that is your mark; you suffered for it; you made it and claimed it as your own. And for those standing around watching, they must encourage that historical sense of identity, celebrate it, rejoice in it and *love you for your achievement*.

And second, if you are going to have children, you must prioritise their sense of

identity over your own. Of course you must –
you have made your mark already, let them
make theirs so that at some future point, they
too can say: There, that's where I come from.
I, the 'me' that is different from 'them'. Even
if the place they are talking about, or want to
talk about, is the same as the one where I
made my mark, it is in fact many moons away
from mine. *Their gaze sees something
different.*

It will be commonplace that the two
senses of identity profiled above will merge
and become one. But in today's instant,
accessible world, it may not. If there is a
disparity between the child's view and the
parents', then you ground the child first and
you never stop grounding them. You can carry
on your preferences in the background: no-
one will take that away from you. But you
never squash your child's dreams and

memories under your foot. Don't abuse them in that way. The consequence is too awful for the child, too terrible to contemplate. *There will be nowhere to bury them or scatter their ashes –*

Easy, lad, easy, said the wheelchair while the Bali Head raised its brow and looked at me. You have made your point …

We set off through the foothills, the wheelchair, the Bali Head and me. We went backwards in time until time got confused and muddled the way we were going. Throughout, however, we set ourselves the task of passing only through the patches of sunlight, pausing in each to hear what the attendant shadows might wish to say. If we had tried to do it in the opposite way – staying only in the shadows – we should never have progressed very far. How to define sunlight? I could think only of memorable things. Like the day the physiotherapy team brought me home to test what I could do. They inspected me in my home, my wife and the pair of us together. But it was sitting briefly side by side in our sunlit courtyard garden that first appeared in my memory. It was simply the act of bringing people on whom I had been dependent to the place which was dependent upon me. Nearly, boy, came the collective voice of my travelling companions: you were simply showing them a completely new part of yourself; and you enjoyed it; you were unexpectedly in control; you were a good host and they enjoyed the occasion. But, a dark voice began to whisper in my mind, they weren't intending to lose control. Furthermore, it was your wife's efforts you were showing off. She surprised you with what she could do while you were absent in hospital. Together, I mused, we extended the warmest, most sincere welcome that we could, by way of thanks for their weeks of care and attention. OK, point made, came a voice from the shadows, that's what you did.

And then before my illness we held a party. A real party with dinner and dancing music and a singer. We held it in the Tennis Club with the river swirling silently by. I loved it. You loved it, echoed my friends because, for once, a substantial crowd had come to you. You were holding out your arms and saying here I am. This is me at this point in time. The good thing, they continued, is that you were giving to them while they were giving to you. Unfortunately it was still your wife they were coming to see not you. You didn't come from anywhere – *there was no-one to invite, nowhere to send the cards to.*

And it was only one evening anyway: we need to look for more like that.

There was no immediately earlier patch of sunlight until one afternoon some eight years ago when I realised that my field was proving more than a normal point of interest for part of the local wildlife. Over the years, I had watched recurring patterns of migratory birds, of badgers, of fox cubs dancing and then of one particular vixen I could still recognise in subsequent years (I decided that vixens probably stay in the local domain while dog-foxes set out for pastures new). On the hill behind my modest patch of Munster was a family of hares. I would go up to see them, disturbing them when I never meant to, wondering what they did and where. For days it seemed, one summer, single hares would make their way down the hillside, following scent-only criss-crossed routes. And then, they would come into the field and start chewing at something always in the one particular place. I would go and look whenever the hares had gone but could never see what they were eating. There was just grass, no weeds, no wild flowers, just grass. I straightened up and surveyed the hillside where my attention was caught by a solitary hare criss-crossing his way down towards me. Stay still, I thought. And I did. Do you know

—

What? chorused my two companions.

The hare came into the field and sat upon my boot chewing the grass around my feet. I could feel ... no, I could *sense* its jaws chewing. I stayed silent and immobile for about ten minutes when my peripheral vision caught movement as the hare returned the way he had come. I looked down but nothing had changed. There was still just grass and a recurring, sunlit memory.

From one afternoon, to one evening, and then to ten minutes, muttered the wheelchair, where next? Be quiet, said the Bali Head, his was a really rich experience. Short but concentrated. How many could claim something similar? But where did it come from, continued the wheelchair. The experience, not the hare. I understand where the animal came from. Oh dear. Confusion.

The experience came from his intrusion into the natural world, explained the Bali Head while I struggled with my spinning sphere of view. Without his action, followed by complete inaction, there came a rare event. I hadn't a clue what either the Bali Head or the wheelchair were saying. But then I thought about it and I did.

But the event didn't begin before his *inaction* had commenced, persisted the wheelchair. There was just grass and him standing there. Are you saying that his experience originated in his non-experience?

If this is still confusing you then I hope you don't ever take quantity of drugs that I have. The necessary pause for thought – like gasping for thought – made me realise that there were really only three patches of sunlight left. The rest, mere dappling light through the leaves of perpetual sorrow, were just things I had done and almost as quickly lost sight of again. I hid in woods as little more than a six year-old, close to a path on which people passed without seeing me. I could merge with natural surroundings like that and briefly drew grim satisfaction from it. I climbed a mountain. I dived naked into an ice-cold pool in a mountain burn. I rolled down a slope of bracken. I rode my bicycle over rough ground knocking myself out when I fell off. I caught my first salmon. I borrowed a shotgun, killed a pigeon and cried, more at the mess than the death. I trudged over a hillside through driving rain and mist carrying a churn for milk when we ran out. Always Highlands, always up there. I dived over the stern of a racing yacht and trod water out at sea until they circled and came back for me. I navigated a frigate. I exploded 'ordnance' – things that were meant to kill. Except I could do things with plastic explosive that produced unusual effects without killing. I learned to fly a helicopter, to teach people how to do it at sea and then to land it facing aft (backwards) on a seriously pitching deck. Only one thing from my aviation career made something of mark in the grand naval memory, the opening line of the written report following an annual simulator check.

Alright, biy, you've told me and I can see that you were rightly pleased.

Can't I say it here? Just once?

Alright, said the wheelchair and the Bali Head together.

[Me] is an experienced pilot but this was remarkable. I was so proud to see it written there: … *this was remarkable.* But then I forgot about it although I did fly a solo display at a very important event. But that was forgettable, too.

Oddly, the three patches of sunlight were really anything but sunlight because shadows waited dominant in the wings. First, as I mentioned earlier, I held my dying father's hand and felt closer to him in dementia-land than ever I had before. Second, I sat beside my dying partner as the cancer squeezed the last life out of her and suddenly realised that I was not alone at her bedside. But more importantly, I also realised that 'they' were standing back, allowing me that one-time space to be with her, and then they advanced and took her away with them. And the third patch of sunlight came six months later, to the very minute, when the world she had gone to made its presence known to me in a most extraordinary, remarkable, inspiring way.

I need say no more of the detail but 'thank you'. It took place in a remote part of Co Galway, Where I was walking over a hillside, but I knew that I didn't come from there. I was merely passing through. They just chose to communicate with me there and at that point in time.

How sad that my three patches of sunlight were all associated with death. It gave the darkened foothills an unnecessary and largely undeserved portent. I relate it back directly to my dreams being erased beneath a jackboot's heel and never allowed to resurrect.

Wot's 'e talkin' abaht now? asked a cockney wheel-barrow. No idea, replied the Bali Head.

They wanted to give me a medal but I wouldn't accept it, I spoke into their silence. (True. Like all the rest of it, it didn't go down terribly well – the return of the medal, not the silence.)

I was mistaken about silence. They had gone. Nothing was left.

Except this time, I was not tumbling. I was not helpless. I had completed the outward bound, half-orbit of my world, or of such sense as I could make of it. And survived. I had learned that, once slammed against the wall, the wall will 'answer back' in the form of companionship and provocation, encouragement to keep going in the search for more. It is simply a question of listening carefully enough for the voice that answers back. Somewhere. Somewhere out there in the dark, is a light waiting to be enkindled. But quite what happens once the spark darts out through the dark toward you to make contact may be anyone's guess but only yours to determine.

The point once again is that 'it' is entirely within your control. It's emphatically yours. But here's the snag: 'it' is, probably, the dark side of you. I cannot be more certain than that. The side you could pass through life without suspecting was there unless you experienced as great a calamity as the one that befell me.

In the early lines of this saga I explained that I had a box which I had marked *Puffs and Squirts*. Well, now I have another one marked *Pills for disposal at pharmacy*. Inside, I have 39 Gabapentin, four Amoclav and assorted tinier pills, all still in their bubble-wraps. At the outset, I was in dread of missing one of my pill 'sessions' (morning, early afternoon and bedtime) but at some point, I discovered that I could miss a session without too much going wrong. And look, in the case of Gabapentin, 39 divided by three makes 13 batches or just over four complete dosage-days of Neurontin. *Four days out of 665 missed nerve pills*. There was also a little pink thing enticingly called Montelukast. The Montelukast doesn't do anything as far as I can see: the state of my chest still terrifies me whether I take it or not.

Now let me turn to that beguiling little phrase "without too much going wrong". Since I started my 'disposal' box, I have learned that, when it did go wrong, it connected me right back with the aeroplane in the field. And with those poor souls running along the ditch. Twice it has done that since leaving hospital. And on one of those two occasions, it opened the door for my Heinrich Himmler look-alike. He turned up here, too. Just three days ingesting mood-lifters out of a possible 665 and he turns up again.

As they say in America: "Do the Math" and wonder what is in those pills – or in the unknown mood-lifters. This is the daily list of allegedly non-mood-lifters:

Zirtene 10 mg FC Cetirizene
Montelukast Mylan 10 mg FC

Gabapentin – mentioned earlier; this is the one which frightens me (9 x 300mgs each day, every day since 19 February 2019, continuing)

Atorvastatin Mylan 20 mg FC

Deltacortril ENT - 5 mg minimum dose, often a further 40 mg would be prescribed for continuous eight day periods

Paracetamol

Nuprin 75 mg Aspirin

Furosemide 80 mg

Escitalopram Teva 10 mg FC

Butrans, one large patch continuously

Scopoderm, one small patch moved from one side of the throat to the other

Plus antibiotics – Amycin, Augmentin, Clarithromycin, Septrim, Gentisone etc

Relvar inhalation powder 92/22mcg, one puff daily

Spiriva Respimat 2.5mcg, two puffs daily

Dymista 137/50mcg, one actuation per nostril daily

So, my life is now defined by prescribed chemistry. Lots of it. In principle, I think this is a good thing: my normally functioning brain and nervous system have been damaged; their intended function is to protect me but now they cannot undertake that task as effectively as they could; therefore a clinical intervention has taken place to replace the damaged function.

Sounds good, doesn't it?

I am not so sure. If the clinical intervention could be tailored exactly to the damage sustained, I would have no qualms. But the quantity of drugs prescribed *already* for me by medical decision has served to make me uneasy. However, unease was never the clinical intention. And now I construe from subsequent discussions with my medical advisers that they will try, whenever circumstances suggest the timing is right, *to reduce* the quantity of drugs that I am ingesting. (In fact, they have already tried reducing the intake of the Gabapentin and had to restore the original dose.) That must mean that they opted for *'a blanket blot-out'* in the first instance – an ugly term by which I mean throw-everything-at-it. And the chemical consequence is demonstrably that things got through which my natural defences would have kept out.

Even though I have been blessed by the quality of my medical and clinical care, I am entitled, for the purposes of this book and for those who might tread in my footsteps, to declare myself profoundly unsettled by the throw-everything-at-it approach. Perhaps that is the state of medical knowledge at the moment and people like me just have to get on with it? But I don't think any of us wants blanket blot-outs or throw-everything-at-it if the consequence is to saturate the mind and nervous system with chemicals, or worse, to compromise its defensive systems. If there has to be clinical intervention, we want and (I think deserve) at least a degree of subtlety, of fine-targeting. *We are always entitled to expect better.* Without it, we'll just go scrip-crazy on top of having a stroke.

So, what did actually happen in my case? I ask that question because, in my case, something did manage to get through the chemical protection zone. For example, my wheelchair squeezed through and I encouraged it. Then it made enough space for my Bali Head to follow in turn.

(For separate discussion is whether 'the need' to restore the original dose is a consequence of my organic needs or of the chemical intervention's separate shortfall. And I could not possibly participate in that discussion without understanding in detail the planned *vs.* the perceived state of recovery in my body and brain – which in turn would appear to require at least one excursion into medical ethics. And who, by the way, is charged with that responsibility in my case? When I did my Ph.D. research I had to present my methods and my intentions to an 'ethics board' for clearance – a distinct external check on what I was proposing to do. But there hasn't been such an intervention: the words 'ethics' and ethical' have never been used in my hearing while in a clinical setting. That concerns me in view of my scrip-intake. So I assume that one of the consultants undertook that task. Who I wonder. And whom did they report to?)

Well, I am quite relieved at having got that off my chest: I haven't regretted either encounter or companionship. But what if none of it had happened? Knowing about this other world of Me, I would have regretted it deeply. But if I didn't know, I would have been none the wiser. I might have turned to Aldous Huxley but his was an adventure with one self-prescribed hallucinogen (and later with LSD). His conclusions were characterised by the intensity of the existence of whatever came into his view – perceptions of surface qualities and then of what lay within. Aldous

Huxley recounts a brief experience with perceived shades of difference not normally seen. My 'adventure' was characterised by experiences laid layer upon layer as I grew and aged. Like rings within a tree trunk. A different thing I think.

My experience under drugs also lasted longer, much longer and can even today whisk me away to half-dreamt, half-learned situations all characterised by darkness. But I don't think the darkness was the consequence of the drugs. They just made my journey within a possibility. The darkness came from me, my experience and my upbringing. And so I didn't turn to him, to Aldous Huxley.

Worth noting is that the drugs in my case, unlike his, have made me hyper-sensitive to one dominant, over-arching unease – the lack of a starting point in this world. But that is just bad luck. I envy those who come from here or who come from there and concentrate on whichever one it was for them. Their scrip will, I imagine, penetrate lighter corners. However, I am the stronger for being from neither here nor there. And I can live with that. My origins lie entirely within: I am more aware of the world within and more respectful of its potential to collaborate with external entities. The others can only suspect the existence of that world while I have already experienced it and concluded that it is a strength.

I have wondered if this means that I am more emotionally intelligent. But I don't think so. Emotional intelligence is focused outwards whereas my experience and attention are focused within. I have learned to celebrate Me – but Me as a consequence I have yet to completely understand. Huxley, citing Pascal, suggests that what I have gained is the power of contemplation, which must be wholly beneficial:

> The sum of evil … would be much diminished if men could only learn to sit quietly in their rooms.
>
> Huxley, *The Doors of Perception*, 19)

Perhaps Aldous and I have reached coherent conclusions? Or perhaps I still haven't completely understood. I am still doubtful, as you can see.

Dear Aldous,

This is a short valedictory written from my apparently 'squalid' mental world. Your word, not mine.

Be under no further illusions, I rather like my world, even under the burden of a 'stroke survived' – a Cross as Christians *might call it. I have come to celebrate what I consider to be its strengths. In contrast with yours, I think, my experience of drugs has made me more sensitive to the objective and dismissively prepared for the relative. You, in contrast, and I am sorry to sound savage, come across as a name-dropper calculatingly damning everything the world beyond those "8 to 10 hours" of mescaline contamination finds glorious and uplifting. If that is indeed the effect upon you of taking mescaline, then I am saddened by your experience. Indeed, I am saddened by the effect that you felt you needed to experiment in the first place. Was it some gap in the effete drawing room literature of the mid-20th century that you noticed and then designed an enquiry to fill? The opportunity of immediate diversion that appealed to your satirical precocity? Or a* *cynical departure in order simply to revive your flagging reputation?*

I am deeply sorry that you suffered throughout your life with problems with your eyes. And if that affliction has in any way heightened what has disappointed me, then I withdraw the severity of my criticism and apologise. But, in no circumstances, could I ever change my underlying opinion. I may have arrogated to myself in the opening sentence of this letter a hint of companionship on our separate entries into the world of chemical impact but I didn't need to. You chose, I did not. We were only ever on different journeys and I never found anything like your 'eternal Suchness' on mine. I only confronted an extraordinary wheelchair who could think, reflect, annoy and talk in simpler terms than you; and my Bali Head who kept me rooted in the world I was being forced to transcend.

Furthermore, I am appalled at your suggestion that mankind would benefit from frequent chemical intervention, albeit a different chemical from yours. What on earth, literally what on this beautiful earth, was so dreadful as to bring you to such a conclusion? Was your experience of life so bad? I think not.

Here, I have to acknowledge that 'bad experiences' reproduced ad infinitum for the benefit of the next generation can be tough on a child. That was my experience and it has affected me greatly even though I think I have emerged the winner. But look at what you said about your ideal designer-drug (my generation's phrase, Aldous, you wouldn't have heard of it). I could never have come out with something so scrip-crazy as this:

... it must be less toxic than opium or cocaine, less likely to produce undesirable social consequences than alcohol or the barbiturates, less inimical to heart and lungs than the tars and nicotine of cigarettes. And, on the positive side, it should produce changes in consciousness more interesting, more intrinsically valuable than mere sedation or dreaminess, delusions of omnipotence or release from inhibition.

Your description of the optimal experience is to me not just trivial and indicative of superficiality, it's downright dangerous. Perhaps that is a reflection of your place in history, of the way things were in a world wrecked repeatedly by war, fascism and totalitarianism. Without wishing to sound precious, I don't think that much of what I have read reflects well on you. I am horrified.

But then, Aldous, finally, you do manage to hit the nail squarely on its head: "The man who returns through the chemical

Door of Perception is not the same as the man who went in." He will have changed and, you say, changed for the better. My main disagreement with you is that I do not believe that a chemical intervention is necessary for betterment and improvement. This beautiful, vanishing world, which my generation is destroying through chemicals, still contains such wonderful, transcending sights that all we need to do is open our eyes to see them and our hearts to love them.

Rest in peace, Aldous. Unless you can change something odious in the world my generation has created, you might find it easier staying where you are. From my perspective, you missed your chance.

Martin Kay

September 2021

A charming nurse brought me a new tilting bed two days ago. And then Himmler came to test it in the small hours of this morning.

After an uncomfortable day nursing a face the shape of a rugby ball (yet again I came off worse), I managed to struggle home from Accident & Emergency, with still no badge for good attendance, at about 2 o'clock this morning. Everyone had gone to bed, steeling themselves for a certain four year-old lady's birthday party today, while I was left to shoot the breeze with a taxi driver from New Delhi. A nice guy but I somehow made the mistake of assuming he was a new arrival. It turns out he had been living in Cork for 12 years and there was I suggesting which was the best route home. I wish the wheelchair was around to stop me but he was nowhere in sight (or sound) and, anyway, I didn't feel equal to explaining to my Indian friend that my best mate was a mobile seat.

So, once again Himmler was the cause of a thoroughly disrupted day – or, to put things in their correct, chronological order, a thoroughly disrupted night, then day and finally evening. I still have a splitting headache, but no fractured skull I am relieved to say, although the effect of his unwelcome influence may yet last longer.

The story is a simple one. Himmler and I began to wallop each other. I lost. And my heavy oak desk played a part in things. So did the left side of my head. And just three or four pills over 19 months ago did, too.

It was then that I began to wonder if Himmler and Huxley shared more than just a capital letter, an age of war, spectacles and a taste for nightmare. Mercifully, the thought was fleeting and better left, I concluded, to those with time on their hands and little else to fill it. I in contrast, I realised, that I had a new sense of purpose.

To help focus my thoughts, I considered first the opening sentence in the most difficult book I have ever read: "Hannah Arendt is pre-eminently the theorist of beginnings."[8] Well, I think I certainly learned things from struggling with her various works but, on this occasion, nothing immediately presented itself as a possible way forward.

I'm sorry. Something unexpectedly did.

"Wot did yer learn then? Wot did yer learn from having to struggle a bit?" the voice needs no introduction.

Where have you been, I wondered.

Speak up! commanded the wheelchair who seemed to have changed shape. He no

---

[8] Hannah Arendt (1998). *The Human Condition*, The University of Chicago Press, from the Introduction by Margaret Canovan.

longer had two big wheels at the back and two little ones at the front but one at each corner with all of them the same size. He still had a seat in the middle and handle-bars with brakes at the back but he was now very much designed for me to propel and then sit down on, not the other way around

Stop starin', he said. This is to get the message across that you are as far from the 'orspital as you can be while still bein' in it. One foot wrong and I shall tell 'em and yer'll be out wiv no comin' back in. (I nearly took the offer but wisely held my peace.).

Anyway, speak up! I can't be doing with mumblin', especially not from name-droppers. You were quick enough to 'ammer Aldous, so start justifying 'anna.

Jesus, where did he come from, I raged quietly before realising that this was exactly the way to go. My wheelchair was right.

If you must know, I replied, I almost shouted, I learned most about Power.

And where 'ave you used that knowledge in this adventure?

Once I realised that his line of questioning was reasonable, justifiable, I found no difficulty in continuing to answer. Being put on the spot was healthy. And it was mind-stretching in a way that my pills were obviously not.

Controlling my wrath as calmly as I could, I said in answer to his question: knowledge … knowledge when explaining how parents can dominate children, especially in the case of children who are constantly uprooted. I said that the parents must stand back and allow their children the time and space to scrabble and root out the rock-face of their own existence so that they can finally say: There! I come from *there*. Not from my parents' 'there' but from my 'there'. And then I said, if you don't stand back and allow them space you are misusing parental power in a way that will damage them and limit their horizons and potential.

'ow doo yoo know? he demanded slowly and accusingly.

Read the previous 25,000 words, I replied quickly and snappily. (I had got beyond both courtesy and caring.) And then, rather obnoxiously and unnecessarily I added: And then you might care to read my explication of Michel Foucault – I think it is better than most.

And then, I apologised … I actually said 'sorry' to a wheelchair, something I could not possibly imagine doing before.

"I apologise. I did not wish to sound offensive. I merely wanted to draw your attention to the work of Foucault on this subject. He is notoriously complicated and I have published something which tries to unravel what he told us. I am sorry. I didn't mean to cause you any offence."

Well then, just in time young man. Just in time oi moight add. As it is, we spent some time on Foucault last month and, oi agree, 'e ain't easy. What about 'annah Arendt? I'm interested. We'll be reading 'er down the Garridge next month.

I was stunned but didn't let on. It was not just that the Garridge 'ad a book club – sorry, *had* a book club, but that someone (something?) had decided that one of the last century's greatest political thinkers should be on the list, and that they had already looked at Michel Foucault.

I was using Arendt to try to establish which way I should be going, I replied at last, towards politics or self-consciousness.

But there was no immediate discernible reaction until: Where else 'ave you used her?

Dissent, I replied confidently. I wrote about dissent. Foucault helped me there as well.

Say anyfink interestin'? (The capacity of my wheelchair to murder the English language bordered constantly between the entertaining and the downright offensive.)

I think so. It was my turn to reply sniffily again: I wrote about the *solitary* voice of dissent whereas Hannah Arendt focused on the *collective*; I called it an existential moment and drew on Sartre and –

Name-droppin' again. Enough. Let's get going again. The middle course, I think. You'll soon find enough self-conscious politicians to trip over.

I don't know about falling over, I responded sharply, but if you carry on laying down the rules, then you and I shall fall out. I stand for the person who says "No!"

Well done, said the wheelchair. Yah won't be needing my services much longer then, will yah?

Nah, I muttered under my breath.

We live in a world where the power of common speech, of verbal contact between men and women, now conforms to different rules. Marketing and economic activity started the change: the digital age and social media finished it. Only one organisational activity appears to have retained its *original* power[9], which is contemplation. That is the prize I think I have found through Huxley and Pascal. Contemplation – the enormously superior ideal of quietness and the space and

---

[9] You will gather that I discount such modern upstarts as 'riot'.

capacity to examine the soul, and to reflect upon its completeness, its distractions and the impact of change[10]. Once this space was closer, earthier and more immediate. Now it is not.

I suppose, I began to reflect, its very sense of remoteness might mean that at some point it becomes tangible, that it is still there, somewhere back there in the place where I first began to contemplate. Contemplation is not new to me. It could be the place I am searching for that I think I can truthfully say I come from. Contemplation must carry its 'place' with it – like a turtle and its shell.

Let's park that one, interjected a familiar growl from somewhere underneath, and concentrate on contemplation itself. Let's understand what we're talking abaht first.

---

[10] The ancient Greeks called it *Theōria*, or experience of the eternal (Arendt, 1998. *The Human Condition*, p.17)

Good advice, I thought but did not say it.

Despite the solitary, calm and peaceful quality that I ascribe to contemplation, I still call it an 'organisational' activity. Today, particularly in noisy crowded today, it is most assuredly an activity needing preparation. Men and women of today need to pause, to think and to plan in order to contemplate effectively. This is to rid ourselves of the background racket, the noise of the 21st century, the mental interruptions, of marketing and economic activity and to make space in our over-crowded diaries. To achieve any of that calls for shape and arrangements. In other words, thinking ahead, preparations and, as a consequence, activity like disconnecting the 'phone and only then, as an ultimate consequence, contemplation. Think of a yoga class. Prepare … relax … silence …

breathing … transcendence … *nirvana*. You build up from simple beginnings, steadily cleansing the place, the space and finally uncluttering the mind. Hard work getting there whereas, not so very long ago, we lived and breathed much closer to where the end of all suffering happened almost instinctively and as quickly. It was proximate and pretty much immediately accessible.

Yer beginning to repeat yerself, said you know who.

I think that's because I want to highlight something Hannah Arendt identified.

Wot? Spit it out and then we can work backwards, he instructed.

We *are* working backwards anyway, I reminded him. Alright. Here goes. Hannah Arendt said:

> The primacy of contemplation over activity
> rests on the conviction that no work of human
> hands can equal in beauty and truth the
> physical *kosmos*, which swings itself in
> changeless eternity without any interference
> from outside...
> Hannah Arendt, 1998. *The Human
> Condition:15*

Strewth, said the wheelchair, I must write that down before I forget it.

I ignored him and continued with my own thoughts. What she seems to be telling us is, first, there is at least one place out there, somewhere where contemplation happens naturally. She calls this place the physical *kosmos*.

OK, said the wheelchair. But what is this *kosmos* lark then?

She is using an ancient Greek word for the physical world – *kosmos*. I'll tell you a bit more about it in a moment. All we need to understand at the moment is that, by *kosmos*, she means the universe, composed as an orderly system.

Wot's that mean then? Composed and that …

Something serene, complete, unchanging and incredibly perfect. But the *kosmos* doesn't have to be only the place where contemplation can result. Thinking about the place you know you come from, for example. It just has to be some orderly, regular, naturally recurring space – something predictable, the exact opposite of chaos, somewhere you feel at peace. It's the opposite of what's inside us[11]. Didn't we agree that we were drifting in that same direction of chaos? And then you said how do you stop it? And how do you know when you've had enough?

---

[11] Nietzsche, *Also Sprach Zarathustra*, from *V. Zarathustra's Prologue*.

That's right, said the wheelchair in rising excitement. Funny thing, I said, funny thing.

That *is* right, I said rescuing the discussion and briefly wondering when. But we may be going a bit too quickly. What she wanted us to understand was that however much we were to try and create such sublime, perfect spaces, they'd never be as good as the real thing, which is why I said *naturally* recurring. Don't waste your time trying to create some instant antedote to chaos –

That's it, cried the wheelchair. Dere's me tryin' to reverse aht and it was all for nuffink.

Well I don't think it was all for nothing. I do believe you can back away from chaos or reverse out, as you put it. You do that with activity leading towards contemplation. It's just that you can't snap your fingers and achieve anything as pure and beautiful as, for example, the *kosmos* just like that.

It follows, therefore, that however much we try to create that space ourselves it is never quite as sublime or perfect as the real thing. But, by turning towards the real thing, we can accept that a condition in which we might begin to contemplate will at some point follow, and will be superior to whatever preparations we have made in effort to reach that point.

Is that it? asked the wheelchair in sudden disbelief. They'll never buy that down the Garridge. Yer making it far too complicated.

Awright, I replied taking over his Cockney twang. 'ere's the rub: no matter 'ow 'ard yer try, yer'll never get nowhere near as perfick as this *kosmos* of 'ers.

'as she got shares in it or somefink?

Nah – I'm sorry, I can't keep this up. No, Hannah Arendt does not have shares in the *kosmos*. No-one does[12]. Anyway, she's dead. She is simply saying that the *kosmos*, as opposed to anything we might create in our attempts to prepare for contemplation, is better in every way we could possibly think of as a means of comparing them. And here is one easy way to test it.

Wot? asked the wheelchair.

Lie on your back, close your eyes, and clear your mind of every interruption and distraction.

May I suggest, ventured the wheelchair in his haughty tone, that a course in empathy might be of benefit? Exactly 'ow am I to lie on my back?

Let go of everything you can, I suggested. Footrests, handles, everything.

---

[12] I recognise that this a debatable point.

Don't use anything like brakes, you don't need them. Just glide until you stop. And then let the air out of your tyres ... let your mind sway ... gently backwards and forwards ... until you come to a gentle halt. Just stop everything. Now, I shall be doing the same thing but lying on my back beside you. And then I am going to open my eyes. I'll tell you when I am doing it so that, together, we can look up at the night sky above us ... the stars. Then we shall be coming closer to the *kosmos*. And this lady, Hannah Arendt, who experienced more things than we can imagine, and who learned from more people we have heard of, is saying that this same celestial landscape –

I must remember that one too, the wheelchair rudely interrupted.

This same celestial landscape is more beautiful than anything we can achieve or even attempt to complete. And look, she says, up there, the *kosmos*, needs no interference from us, it just goes on and on ...

So, wot's the point then?

If it's truth and beauty you are after, and I suppose in that we could include good health, you don't need drugs, pills or prescriptions.

Now *that* the Garridge will find interesting.

Of course, observed the wheelchair in one of his other pompous voices, it's inconclusive.

Why? I asked.

Well, wot if yer don't want truth or beauty? Suppose yer wanted the doors of 'ell like old Aldous there?

Now, look old chap –

None of yer old chap round 'ere, thank you.

I think you may have missed the point of all this. We are seeking the infinite, the inestimable, something we cannot put a price on. Something we cannot even manufacture ourselves although some brilliant artists might come close. Does that help?

Yuss, he said. I got it. If you want a cheap thrill, you can buy it and use it but the pleasure is gone in an instant and your pocket is lighter too ...

Precisely.

But then wot you're saying also means that you are on a different trajectory to Aldous 'uxley. You're not even aiming in the same direction.

Spot on, matey, I cried to the sensation of raised eyebrows from you-know-who. Aldous was experimenting with some drugs he bought. He just wanted to know what happened to his mind after he took them. But I am asking what happens to everything within me that is capable of perception, when I take a greater quantity of drugs under prescription and for a much longer period. He chose to take one drug for eight days and then he tried another one for another short period, whereas I have been told to take a mixture of around 14 drugs a day for about 600 days *continuing*, because someone told me to. But listen now, very carefully, for this is important.

I'm listening.

There is one thing which Aldous Huxley said which also applies to me. Once you take drugs, for whatever reason, and then come back to ... what shall we call it?... reality, to the here and now ... once you take drugs and then come back, you are not the same person. You are different.

Is that wot yo're trying to write abaht?

Yes. I find myself, quite by chance in a comparable situation to Aldous. And I am going to seize this opportunity. And, yes, I am genuinely grateful that you are helping me.

Will me name go on the fly leaf?

No, it will not go the fly leaf and there won't be any royalties either. But you will get quite a profile in the book. And of course the Garridge will too, I added hastily.

So where next? he asked.

Are you happy that you understand *kosmos*?

Yuss, oi think so. It's all the ancient Greeks 'ad to work with. They just lay on their backs in the middle of the night and looked up. They couldn't make anything better or do anything better.

Alright. A few moments ago, you told me to park the idea that I might come from the *kosmos*. And I don't mean literally descend like Superman or Roy of the Rovers.

'oo?

Never mind. What I am trying to say is that, if I cannot satisfactorily identify some point on the planet and say, there, that is where my roots are, then I am entitled at least to lie on my back, look upwards and wonder … up there, up there … … somewhere.

Does that really make you feel better? asked the wheelchair.

Yes, it does, I replied. You have to feel so alienated, so detached, as to recognise and hunger for the need to feel better. And I do.

Yer soundin' a bit precious, yer know.

I really don't care, my four-wheeled friend –

Are you lecturing me? he asked.

Not specifically you but your sense of belonging. Our world is more or less the same but you are part of it while I feel I am just in it. You have friends, relations and family while I have simply events to attend and too many reasons not to. Now, I could go on for quite a while giving you examples of what it means to be on the furthest outer orbit of humanity and you would be justified in concluding that I was full of self-pity. But I am not. I am trying to find words which can satisfactorily describe where I come from.

And the reason for that?

The reason for that is this: everything in this world which you are familiar with is aimed at isolating precisely where you come from; precisely where you fit in; precisely which colour you have on your back; and precisely what accent you should be speaking with. It's capitalism, consumerism and overriding nosiness gone mad. And I am a little tired of it.

Yer in a minority, yer know.

I know, I know, I replied. But it does mean that I can decide what happens next.

Not if yer ain't got wheels, it don't.

And on that point, the conversation ended.

I needed to take stock. I was relatively speaking pea-sized and at the most extreme point of an elliptical orbit with my home and my existence far away at 'the centre'. Worse, I had no confidence that the laws of gravity would keep me swinging predictably and centripetally around the centre and bring me safely home again. All I had … well, was a mobile seat, a seat with four small wheels on. Its padded seat hinged upwards to reveal a small space for shopping and so on, and it had a pair of bicycle handlebars with brakes on by which I could push and manoeuvre the contraption until I decided I wanted to sit down. Even worse still, the thing could speak and had a mostly 'bolshy' frame of mind.

'ere, are you referrin' to me? came a familiar voice from somewhere underneath the seat.

Yes, I replied. I was reflecting on our present situation and counting my blessings, which was only partly a lie.

Don't forget what I told yah, he continued. Yer still on the books of the 'orspital which is why oi'm stuck 'ere in attendance.

Does that mean that we are now going to go back? I asked.

Yuss, he said. And then, unexpectedly, he broke into a quite acceptable rendering of the Corkonian anthem 'On the Banks of my own lovely Lee'.

I even clapped his delivery of those famous closing lines:

> Where I sported and play'd 'neath each green leafy shade
> On the banks of my own lovely Lee.

There, I said, there! There is no doubt at all that you know where you come from.

I agree, he said. Irish by birth and Cork by the grace of God, as that famous footballer once said.

Doesn't that tend to prove what I have been struggling to get across? I asked with a hint of menace.

Orlright, orlright, came eventually a reluctant reply. That's fine by me, guv'nor, said the wheelchair. Where to next then? he asked knowing that I had no idea at all. There was a pause, mostly on my side.

Now look, guv, said the wheelchair at last, I know I've been giving you a bit of a hard time but I reckon we need each other at the moment.

I nodded gratefully.

So, he continued, why don't we next go back to all your mountain tops as you call them. All the patches of sunlight.

And then what? I asked.

Your problem is these pills you've been taking. Let's compare the hilltops now wiv 'ow you remember them ... wiv 'ow you *fink* you remember them. Then any difference will be down to the pills. At least we'll have something to go on.

Good thinking, I said, and thank you.

The wheelchair gestured graciously in response.

And then we set off.

And then we stopped.

We've already done the hilltops, I said. We've already done the sunny bits. And I cannot detect any differences. There was only … well, first, it was that experience of death, of her death … and of the sensation of not being alone. Then, it was my father and the different sensation of being alone. And then it was the wildlife … the hares. There were some other sunny spots, too, but they seem to have passed quickly from my memory. None of them throws up anything remarkable or notable. It's only the dark places that seem to linger. I am more conscious of shadows. They don't come up sharply in my mind unless I decide to focus in on them. Like a zoom lens.

Zoom, zoom, went the wheelchair. I could scarcely believe it. He was doing tight circles and wheelies. Zoom! Dear God: I had a brief vision of hundreds of other wheelchairs doing the same thing too ... there, in the shadows. Thousands of them!

Please behave, I cried as my own wheelchair flashed past. Don't be childish.

Can't help it, guv, he shouted over his left arm rest. It's wot yer said. It took me back into one of me own shadows. Orlright, he said. I've got it back under control – it's like a sudden surge of power in me right wheel bearing. Cor blimey, he continued. It's enuff to take yer breff away.

You've reminded me of another dark shadow – this time in hospital. It took my breath away too.

Wot?

Catheters, I replied. My first catheter. Don't ask any more. And helpfully he didn't.

What 'appened to Aldous then?

Well, one thing he made clear and we ought to remember.

Wot?

[Mescalin] administered in suitable doses,... changes the quality of consciousness more profoundly and yet is less toxic than any other substance in the pharmacologist's repertory.
Aldous Huxley. *The Doors of Perception*

So I don't think he was hopping on drugs, if I may put it like that ... he was barely floating. Most respectably, I think, ...

Sniff, sniff, could be heard somewhere in the background.

Almost respectably, I continued, he was interested in the quality of consciousness and what could just lift him off the ground ... just enough. I think we should try to set whatever my dark places throw up against consciousness. We need to understand what is changing ... what happens to this thing called 'quality'.

This could be interesting, offered the wheelchair as if he was sucking at an empty pipe. Very interesting … I suppose yer want nuffink from me but to keep going and then obey orders?

I agreed. What else could I do? I had no idea what was coming. I could only steel myself for the shadows as each one came up to encounter us.

Well, 'ere's an opening thought anyway, continued my four-wheeled friend. Just as there is an inside to experience as well as an outside, there could just be more than an inside to consciousness.

Very impressive, I cried. Where did you get that from?

The first bit mostly from 'uxley, he said. Yer not the only one to 'ave read 'is book, yer know.

Dear God, I thought. Is there no stopping him?

He continued, scratching and pecking at the pages in his own pocket note-book, and finally reading out loud from a grubby page with pencilled scribble upon it:

> *Visual impressions are greatly intensified and the eye recovers some of the perceptual innocence of childhood, when the sensum was not immediately and automatically subordinated to the concept. Interest in space is diminished and interest in time falls almost to zero.*

'Ere, wot do you fink he meant by sensum?

Anything to do with sensation, I should think, perhaps the totality of sensation. And then (because I couldn't resist it), it's from the Latin you know. The wheelchair was a bit of a show-off, a bit of a snob. So I thought I'd give him some of the same.

All I could hear was a faint grumbling disappearing into the distance, and I turned my attention to the wheelchair's quote from Huxley.

Interesting. It sounded like the young girl gazing intently at her father. I paused and then continued:

Wherever he recorded an impression, it was through the eyes – *visual* impressions, not tactile for example. His descriptions seemed exclusively illuminated for him … lights swelling, expanding and finally dimming … sumptuous colours … he brought new dimensions into the colours he observed but, and this seems crucially important, he never went beyond what he could see. To me, Huxley was indifferent to space and to time – it was colour, new depths and contrasts, new shades and new intensities – not things that were never there in the first place.

A bit different from us, guv', offered the wheelchair. Yoo 'aven't once mentioned a colour to me and, if yoo'll forgive me, yoo seem a little obsessed wiv wot ain't there.

I agree that our experience is different from Huxley. And I recall reading somewhere that he had heard or been told or had concluded, I don't know which, that Mescalin takes you as it finds you. And another thing, he tells us that Mescalin gave him the temporary power to see with his eyes shut. Mescalin gave him that same power to see with his eyes shut but this only lasted for a while. I re-ordered the sentence without really knowing why.

What do you make of that? I asked the bundle of self-opinion I was currently sat upon. And, together, we sat for a while trying and managing to make sense of where we were, what we had learned and the extent to which Aldous and his experiment brought anything to our situation. It boiled down to this:

1. Because I was an old fella (only 74 years, I swore to myself), I remembered a time when experimenting with drugs was risqué and somewhat fashionable. I was an undergraduate at the time and we all knew that a prominent intellect called Aldous Huxley (AH) had written just a decade and a half earlier a book about the doors to heaven and hell. *Dangerous stuff!* I even remembered a medical student – English not Irish, I am relived to say – who used to grind marihuana into her cake mix. *Now that was really dangerous stuff.* (Thank God I never tried her baking.) It followed that I was not writing in isolation; I was adding a brick to the wall of knowledge, albeit

one that really bore little comparison with AH's experiment and was about 60 years later. But that I was following in someone's footsteps was important to me.

2. Notwithstanding item 1 above, I have drafted a very dismissive and almost contemptuous response to AH. I am undecided whether it goes over the top but have decided that it doesn't matter anyway.

3. AH's experiment struck a chord in my mind many decades later. Did his experience offer anything that could usefully be said about my situation – notwithstanding the key differences that his was a limited experiment with very small quantities of one drug whereas mine was a greatly extended experience of substantial quantities of prescribed

drugs? There seemed to be only one observation of common relevance: *enter this world just once and you will never be the same again.* (The sociologist in me thought that so much was self-evident but I said nothing.)

4. As a matter of consequence, any attempt to explore 'this world', as I was doing, must also seek to articulate or otherwise describe the differences as they occurred for each actor. It was almost a responsibility.

Keep going, whispered the wheelchair. You can come back to those ones later.

I nodded my thanks and, sitting as I was upon his seat with my eyes closed and in as perfect a posture as I could manage, kept going.

5. Of some significance were the differences between AH and me. AH entered a world of stunning colours, shades and tints. I entered a world where my personality and sense of self and personal history were just as mysteriously revealed. I shall put that one to one side, too, I decided. The wheelchair harrumphed his agreement.

6. What is not clear is whether my very limited experience of mood-changing drugs could somehow be compared with AH's very limited experience of gently mood-changing Mescalin, and therefore that the parallel experience over 20 months of taking unchanging 'buckets' of pills three times a day was a mere distraction of no consequence at all. At the outset of putting pen to paper, I had assumed that the 'buckets' of pills were

the significant features; perhaps they weren't.

Perhaps it doesn't matter came the wheelchair's considered opinion. If you need to describe a common feature, I'd stick with time and drugs. If it was the bucket's worth of pills for 20 months or whatever it is, they'd have long since blown you out of the water while leaving him untouched. I don't think anyone will criticise you for assuming, on the available evidence, that your short experience of mood-lifting pills was comfortably comparable with his. Yuss, he concluded. Yore close.

Suddenly, my wheelchair was sounding very scholarly and only occasionally like the cousin of a Cockney wet fish barrow.

7. Armed only with uncertainty, I had to decide what should happen next. And

for one moment of clear thinking, I was able to direct an inquisition into the one thing that exercised me – the unsolved question of Me.

8. I had already established certain truths about parental guidance, based on my own experience and did not feel I would have been able to articulate them without having first entered this curious, colourless world of character-stretching and self-examination. So my adventure could certainly be considered a success to this point. But I had still not answered the additional, fundamental question for me, not fundamental for anyone else but solely for me: where do I come from?

9. The question may seem fundamental but is it a question worth spending more energy and emotion on?

10. Assuming the answer is yes, then what do I do next?

11. Because I have a strong sensation of having *set out* on my adventures so far, it follows necessarily that next I shall have to *go back*. But how do I do that and what shall I have to confront on the way?

As I typed the last two questions above, a thought flitted across my mind. Was there anything I could have done earlier that might have put me closer to the answers?

Yer turnin' towards the black patches again, came a familiar growl. (Was that censure or prediction, I wondered. Or perhaps it was warning?)

Thank you, I replied. Thank you but haven't we just discounted the sunny points?. They were moments of great relief but the only thing they did for me was to make me realise that I was pretty strong, pretty resilient, pretty tough and pretty capable. Of the three 'sunny point' events, I would only wish to experience her death again. I did my best by my father. I did the same by the hares. But I could have done better by her, my first experience of death close-up: who could say any more than that they might have handled things better? Anyway, I think we should continue turning towards the shadows. They'll tell us more.

It began to dawn on me that I had never been further from 'home –'home' at the present being the 'orspital as you-know-who called it. Where we were now felt like being a deep-space explorer just passing behind some extra-terrestrial object in the incomplete expectation of eventually emerging on the other side.

I could only compare it with one childhood experience along the line of the hillfoot villages while at school in the Scottish Highlands. I, aged about 10 years, had gone off for the day with my friend (a friend I tried desperately to contact in later years but who was either dead or avoiding me). We wandered up through the Glen where two burns tumbled and crashed through deep gorges before joining in one foaming torrent (my friend came from there and knew every inch, and my local knowledge wasn't bad either). And then we emerged above, in the sunlight, visible once more from the small village below. We walked up steep hillsides, following the line of one of the burns until we reached a long, deep pool associated with one boys' boarding house at our school. Pausing we could see its Palladian lines set out in the extensive grounds some 1,500 feet below. Unconcerned, we swam naked in the ice-cold water. And then we ate our sandwiches and, dry again, dressed ourselves and set off for the highest peak, Ben Cl****.

On the way we met an elderly hill-walker well-known in the area. A journalist, a writer, an explorer, a kind watcher, widely loved and respected, who could see that we were safe. (Even up there, people quietly kept an eye on you.) My mother used to play duets with his sister, one of the nicer things she did. Under the grand piano was a cardboard box with baby owls inside.

Wiv wot? interrupted the wheelchair incredulously.

Baby owls, I continued, young birds. She had rescued them and was hand-feeding them until they could be released.

Yer Muvver?

No, the lady who owned the piano.

Blimey. Oi never know'd anyfink like that.

That's because you never experienced this wonderful, quirky place where I could be allowed to disappear up mountains in the mornings, only to be hunted down by a search party in the late afternoon and taken home for a severe dressing down. Afterwards, my mother disappeared to play duets. The Queen of Sheba. God knows what the owls thought of her thunderous arrival some 18 inches above their feathery, hook-nosed heads but, I tell you, the Prodigal Son had it easy compared with me.

You've 'ad some problems wiv yer Mum and Dad, 'aven't you? observed the wheelchair in an understanding sort of way. I nodded.

He continued: Did you ever hear that bit written by Larkin?

I don't believe it, I thought. They read poetry down the Garridge too. But I didn't say anything.

They fuck you up, yer Mum an' Dad.
They may not mean to but they do.
They fill you with the faults they 'ad …

I can't remember any more, said the wheelchair.

Stop! I cried. You have just said something. I think it's important. It's the line you couldn't remember … I think it should be 'They fill you with experiences they had' or something like that.

That wouldn't rhyme, said the wheelchair. The word's too long.

No, you miss the point, I countered. (A footplate fell off and that was the last I heard from him for at least another page. I understood at last that my wheelchair did not like being corrected.) It's the experiences she filled me with not her faults. She couldn't see her faults, only mine. Remember what I said, she shook me by the shoulders shouting "We were fighting for our lives!" I never did fight for my life and so I had to go through everything she did until she was satisfied that I had experienced enough, suffered enough to stand beside her and *know*.

Know wot? asked the wheelchair.

What they had all been through, I replied and then continued: And what's more, I think only half of what she dragged my imagination through was actually experienced by her. How could she be experiencing war in Europe at the same time as war in the Far

East? I think she and her generation were so deeply appalled, so utterly shocked and so completely terrified by everything that was happening that their mind and sensibilities were completely impregnated by *each and every* atom of cruelty and misery. She did actually experience the War against Japan and some, but not so much, of the other one.

(My mind was racing as my mother's defences and pretences fell aside. I knew them too well. I had lived them since I could remember. Her memories had to go somewhere. And there was only me in the way. Only me ...)

Furthermore, I continued, I think she was even making me take responsibility for what she went through. Do you remember, the cat in her pram and her teddy bear up the washing pole? Take that and that, I can hear her crying because her life experiences were so tough and miserable even from a young age, before war and all that. *Take that!*

Silence fell. I slouched in the wheelchair, exhausted.

Time for your afternoon pills, the wheelchair reminded me. A couple of paracetamol might not be a bad idea either.

And add some extra just for you …, I said.

Wot?

Larkin … the next line in the poem *Your Mum and Dad.*

Very appropriate, said the wheelchair.

And so peace and normality eventually returned. For a while.

It was about now that I realised that meandering through the recesses of one's mind entailed bumping into some very difficult memories. Not great memories but just little sharp stones that stuck in the shoe and caused me to limp and stumble. It was not so much that the pricks of pain upset me but what I knocked myself against whilst falling down. Why that particular event and not another? I remembered being thrown off a ship because the Captain, a submariner, did not like the fact that I, an aviator, had criticised his Admiral also a submariner. This opened up a succession of shadowy events; the glaring, gleaming, bulbous eyes of the Executive Officer closing in for the kill; the damp eyes of a junior member of my Flight when I said farewell; the crushing of my self-esteem when I then took stock; the moment of inspiration when I picked up a sequence of charts which proved a previous lie at the level of Command in the ship I was leaving, and took them with me home; and then the expression in the eyes of those I next reported to and handed them over. They tried to say I couldn't fly but *my* world's greatest aviator checked me out and proved the second lie. The Captain of the Ship went on to great acclaim and was known to crush his crews repeatedly. Once, just once, I met him again: I am sorry, he said. Please come up and see me, which I never did. I see he died this year; I cannot say I am sorry or that I care. Liar. Him, not me.

And then eventually I understood him and that brought me internal peace. Not his death but understanding. It brought me peace inside. The Submarine World welcomed risk: the Aviation World did not. My World had to work from rules *towards* risk or else you would almost invariably lose an expensive aeroplane over the side – and with it, expensive aircrew. Only when a pirate entered the equation, who did not grasp the way the

Aviation world worked, was disaster inevitable.

I said nothing on the occasion that he and I met and I didn't go up to see him. He wasn't worth it. Neither was his Executive Officer. Ruthless, uncompromising 'medal hunters' is the only way I can think of describing the pair of them ... they'd trample on their grannies to get their names mentioned in despatches. Never let go of your sense of self-respect, I said to the wheelchair. Those others, they had respect for quite the wrong things. (I met the same thing once again in another naval context; people out for fame and glory, allowing no-one to get in the way. Dear God. That such individuals should be allowed authority over other people's lives.)

I continued: I even gave back the medal they tried to give me. Not wanted, *I* don't want it, not entitled, take it away, no thank you. No thank you.

I soon realised that if you protect and defend pride in yourself, respect for yourself, call it whatever you want, you minimise the space for incidental things to get inside, to wreck and to distort. That way, you could allow dishonesty to creep in. I do not mean that you become obsessive but that you begin to squeeze out the space even perhaps for instinct. I do mean equally that you could allow the possibility of evil inside. If you have confidence in yourself, you should be certain enough to have trust if your instinct says: There! That's important but that is not. If you are too concerned with yourself, you'll miss some of the things that count and will obsess over the things that don't .

Like all things, It's a fine balance, innit? interjected the wheelchair.

I could only nod, taking quiet pride in being one of very few officers in that particular navy who had given back a medal. I had accepted other awards before this particular stumble but at least my self-respect was intact, and theirs was back in the press, folded away until needed the next time shining toecaps were in order.

And then we turned our thoughts again to finding the way to go home. Here I should explain that 'home' was now a room in my house where I had spent much of the preceding 12 months. I had fallen here and I had fallen there, bleeding over the upholstery on the way down. I had fallen just about everywhere in my room, so I thought I knew it pretty well: thanks to Himmler, I had even tasted every corner. Books lined one wall, my desk was pushed against a modern fire-place which I finally managed to conceal with photographs, more books and a large model sailing yacht. Elsewhere were sofas, chairs and my hospital bed. On the floor was a beautiful Persian rug and everyone who put their heads around the double glass doors said: Oh, lovely!

It was indeed lovely, even the corner where the wheelchair lived, but the radio on the desk was making me wonder anew about my existence. Cocoon, it said. If you are old and useless and have an underlying condition, stay put!

Oh God. I had so many underlying conditions that I dared not put my head above the window-sill. I could only make real sense of it by recognising that my body was securely locked down there and I was probably the safest old cronk in Cork City in the time of Coronavirus. But, as for the present, my mind was floating free at the far end of the orbit sitting in a wheelchair.

Let's stay here for a bit, I said and the wheelchair nodded agreement. And then the wheelchair asked a question I had deliberately hidden in the back of my mind: had I experienced anything more by way of wartime dreams? Dreams that seemed to come from drugs.

Yes, I replied miserably. Yes, I didn't want to tell you.

Himmler picked me up in his car. It was night-time and raining hard. In the shadows beyond the wet pools of lamplight could be seen featureless buildings. Blocks of construction, shapes of infrastructure were just there, square and Germanic. Looming in the damp and darkness. Inaccessible to all but the entitled.

We stopped by one of these anonymous buildings where Himmler disappeared and the car became mine. In other circumstances, I would have enjoyed it, an early Mercedes with a soft top (pulled up for protection from the elements), four doors and a long bonnet. Two windscreen wipers had been replaced by three which were needed as the rain teemed down even heavier and persistently than before. But I took no satisfaction from either the acquisition or the increase. The whole seemed to speak National Socialism. Power and menace. I did not want any of it but I needed the car.

Somehow I got my parents out of one a shelter behind one of the buildings and into the beast. They were not in good condition and their striped tattered rags stank with filth. In the front seat beside me was my Father. My mother sat in the back with one or two others who had also stumbled along beside them.

I drove hesitantly, experimenting with the clutch, which was surprisingly light for such a large, heavy vehicle. I had to find the place where my passengers could join the queue for the aeroplane. And then the car stopped. I had no idea where we were or where to go, and I had no idea how to start the engine again. The most it could do for us was to provide shelter from the lashing rain. All was dark. Nothing moved. No-one spoke.

Despite the terrifying silence and sensation of nothingness outside the car, I knew I had to move to keep us going, to seek help. I told them to stay in the car and that I would take my Father on and then come back. Why, I had no idea. They could neither agree nor disagree, they were already as good as dead.

Picking up a heavy rain-coat from the floor of the car, I got out and ran round to my Father's door. Somehow, with something's help, I draped him around my shoulders and covered him with the coat. My shoes and trousers were already sodden but he at least had the best protection I could give him.

Completely uncertain about the right direction to take, I managed to stumble forward and then walked more confidently having found my balance. I still tripped across various obstacles, however, and nearly fell when we found the kerb along the roadway. Throughout I kept going, desperate to find where there might be some safety for my Father. There was no sensation of being chased. There was no evil waiting to pounce. Nothing horrid – apart from the condition my father was in, that is.

What did unsettle me, however, was the realisation that I had lost the car. Now I did not know where it was, where the way back lay. I did not know where the way ahead lay either. There was just rain and darkness and a tangled, mutilated corpse upon my back. It gripped me around the shoulders, whispering words of useless wisdom.

It was only later, having sunk to my knees, that I realised that the end of the queue, the last person running for safety, would by now have reached the aircraft. There was nothing left for us – anywhere, it seemed.

Nowhere to go. Nothing. It never happened. Nothing would happen. Never.

And I could only turn back knowing that I would soon be never-ed, too. It dawned upon me that this what it meant to be 'disappeared'.

The sensation of being on the edge with nothing beyond is easy to imagine but not so readily experienced. A majority of us in the western world leads comfortable, stable lives and understands 'nowhere existences' by proxy. Every time we walk along the street and see someone huddled in a doorway, we are looking at nowhere existences. Every time we watch some so-called 'documentary' showing dreadful, historical film clips of prisoners lined up or liberated with concentration camp ovens behind them, we are confronted with a void within which existence is not possible. It was never again going to be possible, they said.

"Never again."

And yet the more recent wastes of destruction that are now our immediate impression of the Middle East and near-Asia have replaced in our minds such wonderful images of gardens, art and archaeological treasure. And when you overlay the rubble and ruins with unchanging pictures of dead children and helpless mothers, then it is clear that we are not just looking at the nowhere existence, we are in it. We reached it many years ago.

Nowhere. Never. No existence. Nothing left. Finito. We have reached the end already.

'ow do yoo account, then, for these sunny mountain tops yoo been goin on abaht? came a familiar accusatory voice.

Time, I replied, time and an initially gentle incline turning into a steadily steepening slope but not recognising it early enough. We are not just near the point of no return.

Why? he demanded. 'ow did this 'appen? They'll want to know, yer know, they will certainly want to know.

I did not need to ask if it was the Garridge he was referring to. Clearing my throat, I gave him the best explanation I could. It centred on power and how it works. They tend to get it wrong, I said referring to the text books. They'll tell you that power is the ability to control the decisions others take and the actions that follow.

Well, wot's wrong wiv that? he asked.

It assumes that power is there ... that someone has already built a power base that controls your decisions and actions. And then we waste time wondering what to do about it, how to defeat it. What is far more important is how that process starts. Don't bother about giving it a name at that stage. Just think about someone or something setting out, where no control exists or is tolerated, to acquire power. If you understand that, you can intervene early enough to stop it.

This 'immler yer keep goin' on abaht, demanded the wheelchair. Tell me 'ow 'e done wot 'e done.

I told him that the process begins when someone is given authority over, or authority by, something quite lawful. In Himmler's case, Hitler was appointed Chancellor of the German Reichstag in 1933 – a disastrous appointment viewed from today, but even then very dangerous if President Hindenburg had actually thought about what he was doing.

Wot was 'e doin' then?

He was opening up access to power when he should have been tightly controlling access – but he wasn't strong enough. If he did manage to think back over the previous 13 years he would have seen what Hitler's game was – building his own power base. But, to be charitable, I think we have to assume the President did not. Either that or he was plain deluded or terrified.

Wot abaht 'immler? *'immler'*, not 'itler.

Be patient with me please. It's important to start with Hitler. He was lawfully in a position of power and, under a wretched piece of legislation, could stay there lawfully for the foreseeable future. Think of him as a light bulb that nobody was ever allowed to switch off.

Now we can turn to Himmler. Think of him as a moth. He is a nobody but he does have an eye for opportunity. And when it comes to Hitler, Himmler senses opportunity. So he does what any moth does: he flies towards the light. Now some moths might get burned and killed off. I suppose you could say that they offended the power that Hitler held.

But Himmler was too crafty and careful for that and so he stays close enough to Hitler to build his own power base but not in a way that gets himself killed off. The result now is, first, that you have a light bulb permanently and lawfully switched on. No-one can switch it off, no-one is authorised to switch it off. Indeed, the light bulb can write its own laws saying you will not switch me off. Second, you have a moth in close proximity to the light bulb. Only the light bulb controls the moth's existence and proximity and while it does, the moth sets about building its own power base (in Himmler's case, it was the SS). Until it completes that project which no-one has authorised except the light bulb, everything about the moth can be terminated if only someone can turn the light bulb off or otherwise suspend or supersede its authority. But no-one can – and certainly not the

President. So the moth continues on, doing what the light bulb told it to, and the SS eventually becomes so powerful that it can even continue under its own steam.

What has happened is that the moth has now reached a point where its own little power base, which only ever drew its authority from the light bulb, suddenly achieves a point in its development when it has enough power of its own to continue independently: it no longer needs the strength or resources of the light bulb to continue.

And that process was repeated across the lower echelons of the German Nazi party until there were lots of power bases neither envisaged nor authorised by the President in 1933, but there in position by 1939 with the authority of the one person who was originally and lawfully appointed. Switch the light bulb off now and you'll find that some or all of them keep going under their own steam and continuing to dream up their own dreadful moral codes[13]. Others are not strong enough and so they fizzle out. But the one who was lawfully appointed – he will never fizzle out until someone switches off the central power that authorised him in the first place[14]. That's how power works. Have you got it now?

Yuss, said the wheelchair, I understand. And is that why yer never seems to win when yer fight 'im – e's just got too strong.

---

[13] The most appalling, memorable example is the notice in the ironwork above the entrance to Auschwitz: *Arbeit macht frei*. Ugh.

[14] Here, the central power is the authority of the German State. Clearly, it was about to collapse which Hitler could no longer deny was imminent. But being an utter coward, Hitler committed suicide rather than face judgement. (Anyone wishing to read about the Nuremburg War Trials should include the biography of the late Lord Birkett of Ulverston. Norman Birkett, the best cross-examiner in Britain, was obliged to sit silently while more senior judges fumbled their way through the proceedings and were openly mocked by Goering.)

That could be the reason, I conceded. That or because I have grown too weak.

Please remember, I continued, fight power whenever someone seems to seize it or grow it for reasons which are not clear. Resist them. Fight them! Even if you lose.

Orlright, said the wheelchair, and stop squeezing me arm rests. Yer 'urtin' me.

Indeed, we were both hurting. I could only think of the camps and the striped rags.

We trundled on through the gloom with my prescriptions tucked safely in the carrier bag attached to the wheelchair's seat. I avoided asking him if he knew where we were going: I knew the answer would be. 'No'. And yet I had complete faith in him. That's what happens with a stroke. Unless your immediate trajectory is upwards, you surrender completely to regular sources of help. You might retain enough residual sense of caution to keep new interventions at bay but, by and large, it is the manner of the help offered that will win your acceptance. Take care is my advice. Notice that I only ever had my wheelchair for help and, together, we travelled to the edge of the universe and were now coming back. All the time I was a hospital number, he was never going to leave me until his terms were right. I trusted him completely

These dreams 'ave upset yah, 'aven't they? the wheelchair asked.

I agreed. It's because I don't know when the next one will arrive and because there is a degree of continuity running through them. None of them is completely disconnected from the previous dream.

Wot are they tryin' to tell yah then?

Good question, I thought. That hadn't occurred to me and no-one had thought to ask it any earlier. Sudden thought: don't tell anyone unless you really trust them or else you'll be back on the mood-lifters before you know it.

I turned the question over in my mind and then attempted to share my conclusions. I think the first thing, I said, is about my relationships with my parents ...

They've not been good, 'ave they? interjected the wheelchairs in gentler tones I am sure he had used before.

No, I agreed. We've sorted out the business of not dragging your child through parental experiences so that they never have anywhere of their own to turn to. But there is something else. It's about each of them ... separately. I think my father always assumed I would be proficient wherever he was proficient. And in some respects I was. I could catch a ball, even better than he could. So why shouldn't he assume that I could hit the bloody thing too?

Tut, tut, said my four-wheeled friend, bad language will get us nowhere. Carry on. And then in a reference to his mates in the Garridge, they'll want to know everyfin'.

So, my father focused on his career, and my mother focused on his career too, and between them his career was very successful. And then occasionally, not often, I put a foot wrong and her wrath could be terrible. I think my mother's bitterness surfaced through shame at the shortcomings in her upbringing. There was nothing wrong with her upbringing except that it couldn't afford everything she saw her friends were enjoying.

Wot?

Better education mostly, and smart shoes. She said that she and her brother passed for the Grammar School but they were never sent there. It rankles with her still. That I had to teach her French as a child helping with the washing up is not something she would ever have admitted outside the house. And her way of erasing the memory was to become fluent in French. Better than me.

Reely?

Yes, I said. Completely fluent. And then she told me about her shoes. She could only have tennis shoes. She said she lost friends because of her shoes. Her tennis shoes actually made *me* feel responsible, guilty … Once you start like that it goes on and gets worse. All your fears and anxieties begin to surface like waste thrown overboard, bobbing in the wake. Why do your own personal fears and anxieties not disappear as conveniently?

They don't mate, they keep tuggin' at yer like yer sleeve's been caught on an 'ook.

Spot on, I thought, briefly scanning a sequence of horror experiences, running my mind over them with my eyes half shut. I was on that ship and next I was not. It was almost a year later that I found myself standing at the lectern confronting new commanding officers. On acquaint they were, and there in the front row was one of them. I melted, just broke down. In every respect. And then it happened again, twenty years later, in quite a different setting, but just as embarrassingly. And what is worse is that I cannot clear my mind of them. How can I do that? Can you tell me please, how can I do that?

I fink there's several ways, said the wheelchair after a moment's thought. First, you got to stop bein' obsessed wiv yerself –

But, I interrupted him –

'ear me aht, he said, 'ear me aht. Like I said, first, you got to stop bein' obsessed wiv yerself which ain't easy. Yer was goin' to say that 'avin' a stroke makes it difficult to fink more widely. I agree, he said, it does. I seen many more like yoo and their minds twists and turns like their nerves does. And yer no different. So yer got to make yer mind strong, strong enough to overcome dem dark foughts.

I struggled for a moment to think what he was talking about and then it came to me: those dark thoughts.

And I can't help yer there. Read a book. Take up yoga. Do somefink for yerself.

Scolded, I kept quiet.

Next, he said, yer wants to join a club or find an activity, somefink to take yerself out of yerself. Yer very close, my friend, to self-pity so snap out of it quick. And then there's religion. Take me, he said, oi'm

Hindu, we all are, down the Garridge. We don't like being told what the story is, we like to work it out for ourselves, to discuss it. Oh yuss, he continued, we also believe that something divine is present in each of us. He paused, sniffed and then begrudgingly concluded: Even in yoo – yoo might like to try it. It's a way of life. Dharmha ... that's how yoo could sort yourself out.

I gasped but tried not to show it. That the participating members of the Garridge should also have a belief system was staggering. And that they all might believe in the Hindu way of life was ... well, tucked away down here in Munster ... well, beyond my expectations.

Do you believe in the Lord Shiva? I asked recalling something from my childhood.

Yuss, he said, but 'e's not SIPTU[15] so we keeps our distance.

And that, the reference to SIPTU, was the first clue for me that we might soon be turning for home. Oh, Lord, thank you.

I could not imagine how the hospital's errant wheelchairs would all be gathered in for the Garridge – for anything other really than storage.

In the background, I could hear something clearing its throat. A warning …

Briefly, I had an image, drawn from waiting in the car park disabled slot outside Dunne's Stores, of someone pushing a long line of snaking shopping trolleys. But I couldn't see that that would work: if my wheelchair was anything to go by, they would

---

[15] The Services Industrial Professional and Technical Union: the public services union in Ireland.

never decide who would be first in the line –
or last so that they could control all the others.
And how would they fit together anyway? So,
I quietly decided to say little, observe lots and
understand as much as I could about this
little-known dimension of CUH Portering
Services – of that and the interface with
Geriatric Medicine which is where it seemed
that our paths had come to cross.

My first thought was that much more
could be done to brighten them up. The
wheelchairs, that is. Do you know how to
recognise a nurse from the children's ward?
You look for the brightly coloured tunics. It's
standard practice across the length and
breadth of Ireland and just about every other
advanced country I ever went to and had the
time and opportunity to notice. Lots of
colours, lots of pictures. Well, my idea is to
find out how many wheelchairs there are in

each hospital and how many sports leagues and divisions we have and allocate a team colour to each one. And then I would go the local colleges of art or to any other useful group of young people and ask them to get painting. I would want a wheelchair in Munster[16] colours.

You've got one if you only took the time to notice, came a disappearing whisper down one of the cheerless unmarked corridors surrounding us. And that summed up our present situation. Which corridor? Which set of colours? Where? Where was I meant to look? The choice was endless and my deficiencies just as troublesome too.

And then something unusual happened. I had another dream last night, another dream

---

[16] Munster is the south west province of Ireland. While each of its six counties has its own colours, by 'Munster colours' I am referring to the provincial rugby team. Their colours are red with a dark blue collar; on the left shoulder is the badge of Cork and on the right a sponsor bade, currently Adidas.

in the same grey, grained sequence, but I cannot remember what happened. For the first time since my stroke, I could not remember what the dream had been about. All I can tell you is that I was working in a hospital environment … but that's all. I was using my energy for the benefit of the hospital. But that was all I understood. That was all.

I am also sleeping better. Dreaming better and sleeping better. All in all, calmer. The dream has not bothered me in the slightest. And so, we rocked and rolled onwards up and down the country track ruts, each quietly musing with our own thoughts until my wheelchair broke the peace.

The time has come, biy, said a rich Cork accent in my undamaged right ear, to come with me to the Garridge and meet my circle of acquaintances – professionals we like to call ourselves. You'll have to mind your Ps and Qs. They'll have lots of questions and they'll push you hard.

I turned to stare at him. Were the surprises never going to stop? Evidently not, as he just kept rolling along. It's my impression, I offered him, that we were a long way from the city of Cork. Surely things could change between now and then?

Oh no, he replied, oh no. It's just around the corner, a bus ride at most. Have you got your card? he inquired. And then, with wink, he continued, I go free. One of the better deals we have in and around the City. Even works in the Bishopstown Municipal Library, I might tell you. (It occurs to me that you won't know how a wheelchair winks. Use your imagination.)

The news that my wheelchair used the Municipal Library came as no surprise. I should think he bought his clothes in nearby Penney's, too.

The cry 'we do, we do' seemed to echo briefly in that barren place, until we were off again.

The wind rushed through my hair, beating my face as we whished and whooshed our way over mountain tops, through dales and up the nearby hillsides towards a nearby bus stop. I shouted at him to stop or at least to slow down. We were going at a breakneck speed – like a movie reel held in reverse and at maximum speed. And through it all I saw the painful memories, *my* memories, dropping to either side, wasted in the dust with all my other anxieties and self-pity. It was a climax to our adventure. But all shown backwards. I was literally being shredded of pain and sore and blemish. Ripped from all that old feeling of hurt so that only the fact of my stroke and the power of my mind remained. Why take them away? Do not take them away! I cried, for they are Me now. I am nothing more than some good memories, some great experiences and the sensibility to use them wisely. I knew at last where I came from. I came from the moment, from the mind and from the flash of energy that made me. Unlike others, I needed no fixed space upon this earth. Luckier than I, I thought – no, not as lucky. Who cares? I decided. I am me. I am the here-and-now, the moment, and I had to use each moment well.

And glowing with such new understanding and excited by its promise, I rumbled – I am sorry – we rolled our way on to the bus where they have a flap that lowers and a man who smiles and works it all. He comes from the moment, too.

We proved our credentials to his satisfaction although I noticed that the wheelchair seemed to avoid showing his. Anyway, we were soon on board and off we rumbled and rolled again under the power of a Spanish engine and with the flexible guide and similar glide of its automatic drive. Wow!

Everywhere I looked there was moment. Pace and moment. We were all sharing in it. Participating. Contributing. Adding to the whole.

I do not know how the bus managed the next stage of our arrival at the Cork University Hospital but somehow it did. I can only really remember squeezing my eyes as closed shut as they would go as, pinned (or bolted even) to the front of the bus, my wheelchair and I zoomed –

Zoom! Zoom! I could hear echoing faintly in the distance.

– into the hospital campus, round to right, o-Oh! just missed Maternity, and then up to A&E. No registration for us, I can tell you. Round to the left we went, pushing our way past startled coffee-boaters, beeping the horn as we warned our way into the bowels of the building.

Warned? Yes, warned. We needed to tell them all that we were coming. Fast and loud. Honk, honk – we are coming.

And then we stopped. And you could see the tiny pieces of dust and debris slowly settling earthwards where our wheels had skidded to a halt.

Sudden silence. Quiet. But too quiet for emptiness. There were eyes watching … well, I think they were eyes.

Slowly, the darkness lifted and what had seemed to be eyes turned out to be wheel hubs. Row upon row of shining wheel hubs. Wheel hubs on wheelchairs. All parked neatly with their foot plates fixed uniformly at exactly the right position. Nothing was out of place. The sweet smell of WD40 laced the air and swirled lazily with each salute of their flexible arms. Rippling salutes down each rank until all had confirmed their allegiance. *This was the Garridge!* Speak carefully, I thought, it is like some Munich rally of the 1930s National Socialism movement. Oh dear, this is where he grew up. At least there were no flags or swastikas. Just uniformity. Normalisation.

What do you mean by normalisation, boy? The challenge came from somewhere on my right.

Please, do you mind if my wheelchair could be released from the front of the bus before I explain? I asked.

Don't worry, he has. He is already in second-line servicing. This was a gruff but not unfriendly reply. And, although I tried to peer into the dark corners, I could not see him. But I could hear a familiar voice, somewhere nearby, shouting Ooh! and Ow! amid the taps of hammers and sounds of something worse.

He has been a wonderful companion, I explained. He has advised me and guided me. I could have had no better assistance. Your wheelchair has become my friend.

At this there was a general sigh of satisfaction and the wheel hub eyes all wobbled briefly with emotion. (They looked ominous, I thought to myself, all lined up like a Nazi parade but they were just a bunch of softies pretending to be tough. Take care, I continued to warn myself – just remember how law-abiding clerks, each one of them supposedly a softy, were turned into concentration camp guards.)

Can you tell me what happens now, please? I wasn't entirely sure how I was going to be able to move safely without my wheelchair and I was rather anxious to move on, to leave the Garridge.

Well, they said, the next stop is Triage —

But we want to hear how you got on and what happened, interjected a new voice. And we want to hear about this normalisation of yours. Come on, tell us everything.

This came from the wheelchair at the end of the nearest line. He glistened with self-importance and his position in the rank. He was evidently senior. And from further down that same front row, another spoke up in a kindly tone: Take your time, there's plenty of time.

D o you think I could begin with this question of what is normal? I began a little hesitantly. There was a grumble of agreement.

I think I must have been thinking aloud, I started. It was just seeing you all here lined up, waiting after being cleaned and serviced, waiting to be sent out again into the hospital to help patients who could not help themselves – and on behalf of patients in the hospital can I just say a quick thank you?

There was a sense of oily satisfaction. Light oil, like soldiers might carry in their knapsacks: squirt some WD40 in the air, you'll know what I mean. It oozed along the rows until all were looking and sounding satisfied. They even glistened with it.

It was normal and reassuring. Just what you would expect from any hospital Garridge. Once again, there was a rumble of agreement. One or two foot plates fell unthreateningly to the floor. Pick 'em up! snapped the senior wheelchair whom I noticed they referred to as S'arnt Major!

The exclamation mark was important: S'arnt Major! Soon there was peace again as each dropped item was recovered and clicked back into place. Peace. Normal.

One thing troubled me, I continued, as we went on our adventure. It was these repeated dreams with War images in them. Fascism. Himmler. Camps. You know what I mean. Not nice. Well, at the root of all that is normalisation.

What? interrupted the S'arnt Major! who liked everything to be normal.

What? echoed the wheelchairs who were evidently cautious about him. What, what? The ones who weren't frightened, or at least appeared not to be, stayed silent.

Choose your words carefully, boy, I thought to myself before continuing:

If you have a group of people – it doesn't matter what sort provided they associate with each other and identify with each other – then certain things tend to be come *normal* within the group. (I gave heavy emphasis to the word to try and make it clear that the last things I was talking about were wheelchairs. I noticed that the S'arnt Major! was leaning forward against his brakes. Slightly ominous, I thought.) Even things that are said and how they are said become normal, expected. And some things are not welcome because they are not normal, not expected.

Now, let me make it quite clear that there are two sides to this particular coin. Groups or associations *normally* work very well – there's that word again: normal, normally. Look here at the Garridge. What better example? (The S'arnt Major! leaned back. Good.) You all know what works best. You normally line up the wheelchairs over there … and along here. You have your own ideas about what is right and no-one knows better. You all help each other and the hospital patients are the beneficiaries. Do you know the very first words that my wheelchair spoke to me were that you all shared one moral truth, that everyone in hospital should have their own wheelchair. I commend you. I commend the Garridge. You are all exceptional.

The heat had gone out of the moment. They all relaxed. Most important of all, the S'arnt Major! had puffed himself up with self-importance and was now polishing some imaginary dust off his imaginary medals.

Now, that was the first side of the coin, I continued. Let's turn it over and consider the other. Just suppose that certain practices within the group attract a certain importance. For example, suppose it becomes not just accepted but punishable if you do not comply (at this, the S'arnt Major! seemed to pay closer attention). Just suppose that it became normal, and punishable for failure, that each member should raise their right arm every time a certain person passed by and shout *Heil!*

There was a silence as each individual in the Garridge reflected on the brief, unwelcome image of nascent German fascism.

Can you see where that sort of thing might lead? I asked, and then with a slightly threatening note in my voice and before they could answer: Ultimately it could lead to railway trains and camps and, for those who are not considered 'normal', to ovens. To ovens, I repeated allowing my voice to trail off …

There was a longer pause but, before anyone could raise their voice, an authoritative tone penetrated the gloom: Orlright, said the S'arnt Major! who betrayed a friendly trace of Cockney in his accent too, now let's move on. Somefink different. What else 'ave you learned?

And so I told them about my endless quest for an answer to the question of my roots: where did I come from? I, who felt so isolated in a world that was so certain of itself, where did my roots lie? And then I began to explain my concerns about allowing young people the space to understand themselves and not, emphatically not, to burden them with their parents' inhibitions and expectations. Once underway, I can be a relaxed, easy speaker and I enjoyed describing our adventures. I managed to keep the theme of Nazi Germany quietly in the background but I didn't avoid it altogether. How could I when I had been plagued by Matey Himmler for much of the last 20 months? At least I raised a laugh when I told them about the battered, bloody upholstery. When wheelchairs laugh, it is like wheel spokes clattering against each other. And generally, I think it is fair to say that they enjoyed what I had to tell them.

But I saved the best to last. I told them what it was like to have a stroke. I took them through each day and night of it. I explained how I had felt able for the monotony. Indeed, there was very little that was monotonous as far as I was concerned, thanks to my family but mostly thanks to having a lively imagination and if that sounds arrogant I do not intend that it should. But then it was also thanks to my wheelchair friend who came 'out of the shadows' as I think I put it all those pages ago. When you have had a stroke, your friendships forge anew.

Where is he? I asked. Still being serviced, they said. Ow! Ooh! I could hear in affirmation.

What is his name? I asked. He never told me.

There was a pause which grew a little longer.

Ennerbryce, came a murmur eventually.

Ennerbryce? I asked incredulously.

Yes, Ennerbryce. What's wrong with that?

Oh oh, that touchy sensitivity again.

What an unusual name, I replied quickly. What a lovely name! (God knows what the rest of them were called, I thought quietly to myself.)

I imagine that you will not have heard a roomful of wheelchairs relaxing in relief. It's halfway between a crunch of digestive biscuits stood upon by mistake, and a tinkle of thin brittle wires crackling under one last squeeze of pressure. Ennerbryce ... I think they were genuinely pleased that ... that I ... mmm ... that I liked it.

I haven't heard that name in Cork before, I continued. Shut up you idiot, I thought. Don't say any more. Not until you've thought about it anyway.

No, you won't they replied. It comes from Waterford. He came from Waterford. A while back.

It's Viking, ventured another hesitantly and at last.

There didn't seem to be anything else to say after that. Either to agree or not.

Someone had to break the silence which was becoming uncomfortable. I mean, the next questions had to be: "And what is your name?" "And yours?" This might quickly take an embarrassing turn, I thought, especially when it comes to the S'arnt Major! (let alone me). And so I took the initiative and stepped forward into … into … well I can't call it the limelight but certainly into the space that had opened up in the middle of the Garridge.

I began: I am very conscious that I took Ennerbryce away … well, he took me away for more than a year and a half. I feel I owe you a more complete account of what happened to us. After all, you – well, *he* made it very clear to me that he had something of a mission. You all feel very much endowed with a purpose …

I could hear the whisper being shared among them: *endowed with a purpose ...* purpose ... purpose ... finally, it disappeared into the distance.

Yuss, said the S'arnt Major! importantly. That would be correct. We are endowed with a purpose, a *group* purpose.

Importantly, he puffed up his chest. I almost heard the medals clink. The message he was conveying was: I am the purpose, I am the group. ('Gruppenführer!' was the thought that came irresistibly into my mind).

Well, I continued, Ennerbryce fulfilled that purpose admirably and he deserves to be commended ...

Oooowww! came echoing faintly through the corridors. Ow! Ow! Ow! could be heard in short staccato cries subsiding finally into a long drawn-out, sobbing moan, Ohhhh!

But as he isn't here at the moment (here, I swear I heard the muffled sound of a wheelchair grunting and squeaking, as if it was trying to wriggle out of chains and padlocks, but I cannot think of any way of describing the sound), I'll tell you some more of our adventures together.

At this point, there was the unmistakeable impression of a room-full of wheelchairs settling down contentedly. They like stories, I thought. Wheelchairs like listening to stories. Now there's a thing to remember for anyone going into hospital for a while. Tell 'em anything and they'll love it. I bet they gossip.

I won't tell you anything about the hospital, about here in this hospital, because you know all about already. But you may not know about St Finbarre's.

We do! We do! they cried. We've been there lots of times.

Well, you may not know about it from a patient's perspective, I responded cunningly, craftily but without thinking what on earth I would tell them. And then it began to come to me. I began with the walls and told them how I was quite certain that walls soaked up the emotions of the people who lived their lives leaning against them.

I suppose that also goes for wheelchairs which are lined up against them? I wondered, speaking aloud and choosing my words carefully. I think the important thing would be intensity of emotion. So, if you had a lot of wheelchairs like here in the Garridge, they could produce the same or similar intensity as one or two single personalities sat on the floor and leaning back against the wall provided they opened their hearts and mouths enough and filled the space with whatever was moving them.

Moving them? asked the Garridge *en masse*.

Motivating them, I replied, their emotions. And then, sensing that I was running out of ideas, I began to tell them about the ancient aeroplane. I soon learned something new which on reflection, once you have recognised what had happened, is a wonderful thing. If that sounds odd, please stay with me. I tried to explain about canvas to wheelchairs (creatures?) who had no concept of canvas. Plastic they understood. Metal too. The idea of curtains brought me close because they could see that fabric was woven and, although I had no idea all how canvas was made, it seemed reasonable to think that it was loosely woven, bigger strands of coarse fibre, natural fibre. So, they just about got it in the end but not completely. Wax was another area of difficulty but oil was not. So, working hard and thinking quickly on my feet, I managed to get the idea of early canvas aeroplanes across. They had seen magazines so engines, wings and aircraft were not difficult either.

But then came a huge challenge. Explaining the concept of war. If I didn't get that across, how could I possibly explain my uncomfortable dreams and the horrid, hateful, recurring theme in my thoughts of German fascism. How could I explain this appalling presence in the corners of my mind of a man called Heinrich Himmler?

And then it occurred to me that standing in front of one audience which had no experience of what I wished to tell them was no different from standing in front of another in comparable circumstances. Wasn't that the challenge and the art of teaching? The only possible difference lay in the maturity of the audience … their ability to understand complex issues.

I began to think these thoughts aloud which gave my words, I think and hope, a freshness and a spontaneity which I believe they found attractive and entertaining. But this in turn led me on to my favourite subject, power, and it was not clear to me how much Ennerbryce had passed on my ideas. If they went to the Garridge for a top-up (his words), could they also go there for a top-down? Did Ennerbryce just plug himself in and 'dump' everything I had said in his hearing? That would mean that I could have few secrets from them. Do not think this is fanciful stuff. If every hospital wheelchair in Ireland, anywhere for that matter, shared the same disposition, that every patient will be assisted and supported to the extent of having their own wheelchair, then they know the personality they are carrying better than you think. Take note of any distinguishing features every time you sit down in one of these contraptions (there was an immediate clatter of falling footplates but, bravely, I continued with my thoughts and there was no further noise or interruption). Be very careful indeed if you see those same characteristics again.

The same wheelchair? A similar one? The first one's mate? Do they talk to each other? Where do they go at night? Remember my question about gossiping. I can hear them now.

Ennerbryce was baffled by the recurring theme in my dreams, I began, this business of wartime prisoners, especially in connection with Nazi Germany and by the sensation of being stalked by Heinrich Himmler. But I don't want to let that dominate the story of our adventures because our time together was wonderfully life-changing. In contrast, everything to do with those war-time images was a wretched glimpse of an horrific period in 20th century life, confronting the disgustingly cruel tendencies of those with power and no sense whatsoever of accountability for their actions. I know now why it plagued me so – 'stalked me' was how I put it just now. It was because the detail of that second dreadful war in Europe tormented my mother more than anything. She suffered a different, shocking youth experience, of brief internment in a Japanese camp. But on release, after it all was over they were sent to hospitals in Australia. She eventually found her way, with me, back to her home in UK.

It had never been a happy home for her: she was bullied … she was … well, nowadays I suppose we would say 'abused' by which I mean pushed around, denied opportunities, shoved down pathways which she considered beneath her. Almost but not quite maltreated. But there was one thing she could never avoid or turn away from. It was still everywhere around her in ruined, bomb-shelled Europe. It was the ability of man to go to war. Later, much later, I read as voraciously as she did and discovered concepts like totalitarianism (thank you, Hannah Ahrendt, I thought under my breath) and the ability of something as apparently harmless as 'normalisation' to trigger waves of group thuggery.

Here, the S'arnt Major! appeared to shrink a little into the shadows of the Garridge.

But whereas I saw concepts and theories, my mother saw something different. She saw person to person violence. "Here we go again", was how she remembered my Grand-father's reaction when War was declared in 1939 but I think he was remembering too many starts of war … the Dardanelles, Gallipoli in 1915, Dublin in 1916, the Somme in 1916, and so on and on and on. Endless war. And only beloved Dublin was the one he missed and what side would he have been on then?

For her, however, it was different from her father for we all carry quite different memories of violence out-bursting. Private memories which no-one else of us will ever understand. We can only offer the ones with private memories time to not understand.

Afterwards, my mother had known and remembered Jewish friends who were no longer there. She told me about groups of people gathering on street corners all wearing brown shirts. And carrying banners and sticks. Ready to get rough with passers-by. Posters with slogans and always with those sticks. Slogans saying hateful things. These were people she had grown up beside but their characters changed in front of her eyes. And they never changed back.

She bled from the memories more than she did from careless cruelty in the Far East. And because I was there after it all was over, like a teddy bear on a washing line, or a cat in a doll's pram, I was going to experience it all too. Take that! And that! She made sure I experienced as much as she could manage. And that!

I don't know who cried loudest.

"The person coming to dinner tonight was caught and tortured ... Make sure you are afraid enough – *before he comes* please."

Together, we waited and sobbed out loud for him.

And because I had had the worst excesses of German warmongering pushed up my nose, it always kept appearing there. Its pain and ugliness stained every idea and space I could conjure up in my poor little vicariously damaged psyche. I alone felt I knew the answer to Hannah's dark question: what turns law-abiding clerks into concentration camp guards?

After a pause, I lifted my head and asked: Does any of what I have said make sense to you?

Yes, biy, said a familiar voice. Doesn't it lads, he shouted to the assembled throng of wheelchairs. Doesn't it!

Yes! they cried. Yes! Yes! Oooowww! Ow! Yes!

I stared at Ennerbryce who sat there, his tyres pumped up shining from top to tail after his recent service. He looked immaculate.

Ennerbryce! I called. I have missed you. I have missed you so much.

And I have missed you, biy. You don't need to be worried anymore.

It's not worry, Ennerbryce, I replied with my voice scarcely rising above the noise of rowdy wheelchairs. *It's fear*. It's fear that turns them into concentration camp guards. Fear and a moment of … a moment of … let's just call it a moment for decision. Fear works away inside you like a worm. And if a parent was frightened and does not allow the child the space to amass their own experiences, they will impress their own fears quite unjustifiably upon the child. They love the child too much to allow good sensations to enter: they can only allow it to experience fear because their own fear has to go somewhere. That's what I mean by a moment. A moment for a clear decision, based upon their own experiences. That's what I think and that's what I have tried to show you.

And how do you think we should use this analysis of yours young man? asked the S'arnt Major! gently leaning towards me. And then continuing: I can see how I may have got a little carried away myself – a lot of course, just a little – but in the way we treat patients in the hospital.

I think you are doing very well already, I replied, but there are two things you could do.

What? they cried in unison.

First, recognise that I shall need wheelchair assistance for at least another 6 months, to which there was a general murmur of approval. "The same wheelchair", I heard one of them shout, to which I immediately and thankfully agreed.

And second, ... (I drew out the moment of decision) ... *promote Ennerbryce to Corporal!*

'ooray! 'ooray! could be heard echoing around the Garridge. Three cheers for Corporal Ennerbryce! (which thunderously followed). And at this there could be seen a small tear in the eye of the S'arnt Major! whose name, most curiously, also turned out to be Ennerbryce.

And after all that, we filed our way down to the coffee-boat for refreshment. The Sarnt Major! led and Corporal Ennerbryce and I brought up the rear. Very satisfactory, I thought. Very satisfactory indeed.

Not long after I reached this point in the story, they discovered that I might have cancer. Not definite of course, just might. After that the experience of stroke faded quickly into the distance, although I continued to tumble about my ground floor room with regular monotony. Backwards and forwards I went into the hospital and various clinics too. And Ennerbryce was waiting there mostly when I arrived. I say mostly because once or twice a young shiny wheelchair took his place. I could see Ennerbryce in the background keeping an eye on his young charge but being a natural leader of wheelchairs, he always stood back and kept his distance. He was after all a Corporal now which made it essential to keep an eye on those under training but not to come too close.

One day I asked the young wheelchair what his name was.

Ennerbryce, he replied proudly, like my Dad over there.

I pretended to be surprised although I had half-guessed the truth already.

I hear he is a very special Corporal, I whispered, much decorated in the field.

Oh yes, said the youngster enthusiastically. He even went on an adventure once. We don't do them anymore, he finished sadly.

If you are as courageous as your father is I am sure an adventure will come your way in good time, I said. Did he tell you anything about his?

A few things, replied young Ennerbryce thoughtfully. He used to go on about people with power and how I had to keep an eye on them … even stand up to them if they got too big for their boots. But it was what he didn't do that I liked most.

What do you mean? I asked, what he didn't do.

Not like some around here, he said quietly, my Dad never crowded me. I always felt that he was standing back … 'letting me make my own mistakes' was how he put it once.

One more question I said to myself, just one more and then I'll shut up. Now I think I am right in saying that your Dad is from Cork here, is that right?

Oh yes, he answered, and he is very proud of it.

And what about you? I asked. You must be from Cork, too.

I am, he said, but I always feel very close to the sea out there as well. Dad let me go to sea once on a sailing ship designed to take people in wheelchairs. They hoisted our chairs up and down the masts with sick people in us. I loved it. *They* loved it, which was even better. So I feel I'm part a sailor, too. A Cork sailor. Up a mast I went. With my patient. And I brought him down again.

You'll be a great navigator as well as a seaman, then.

Just watch me. he replied keenly. *Just watch me*. Where are we going first?

Once round the ground floor – for old times' sake. Then to Ophthalmology and after that the Orchid Centre. And finally to wherever they do colonoscopies.

Crumbs, he said. There seems to be quite a lot wrong with you.

No, I said. There's not a lot wrong with me. I once went on an adventure with Corporal Ennerbryce over there and I have never been better since.

Crumbs, he said. And then called, Dad!

But we were long gone before the Corporal of Wheelchairs came to investigate. And all he found was a pile of pills, discarded as if they were no longer necessary. Only the big orange ones called Gabapentin, which are important for people like me, seemed to have been taken. Far more of an adventure, I think, than anything that friend Huxley's experiments with Mescaline ever produced.

Yes, I agreed with myself as we whizzed along one of the corridors, away from where we had dumped the pills I could no longer stomach. All very satisfactory. Very satisfactory indeed.

A few weeks later, a week or two perhaps, I was sat beside my window looking out at the world as I could see it from my world of desk and books. And it occurred to me that my opening purpose had been to respond to Aldous Huxley. Having blasted him at the mid-point of my journey, it seemed courteous to pay him a re-visit.

Except for those who had lived their lives in the world of hookahs, his was a relatively drug-free world. One of the big discoveries at the time was a substance, an active ingredient, called Peyote which came from a Mexican cactus; and Mescaline could be extracted from Peyote.

The critical feature of Peyote was its ability to change the quality of consciousness through its ability to impact upon the central nervous system. That was the background situation against which we generally understand friend Aldous. No evident corollary with me, you'll note, unless Peyote came somewhere into my own background chemistry. But then it became apparent that each of us could produce a similar effect – an impact upon our nervous system. This was some tiny trace of 'something' that we could produce with an effect that was not dissimilar to schizophrenia.

Now, note here that I have been reporting the recollection of some tiny trace of 'mood lifting' drugs that I had been given on one or two occasions in hospital and which I felt had something to do with my wandering fancies. Wandering fancies? Well, the phrase will do. You know what I am referring to. And I am suggesting to you that here may lie the connection with Aldous Huxley. Perhaps the mood-lifters were triggers or acted in some other way?

Aldous was interested and found himself in a position where he could willingly participate in order to build more understanding. If my own understanding is correct, he took on one occasion the equivalent of about 40% of my daily intake of Gabapentin in the form of Mescaline. And then he sat down to wait.

The result was different from what he expected. It was certainly colour-affected but was more usefully associated with something he called the realm of objective fact[17]. But what *he* meant by that is far from clear to me.

So, exit Huxley. The word 'fact' points in quite different directions.

'Facts', as such, are sociological concepts for their measurable quality. But I

[17] *The Doors of Perception.*

think that Huxley was more drawn to their quality of objectification than to them as objects – simply because he said so.

Yawn. Yawn, yawn, yawn, came pointedly from the corner.

Alright, I cried. I'll keep it brief.
What he means by objectification, I think, is:

> the ability of the human mind to envision its existence in the world it has created as its biological life unfolds.

Wait! came a not unexpected interruption from the corner, followed by the sound of scribbling and squeaking as notes were taken with a frequently sucked pencil stub.

Now that made sense for me in my analysis of where I came from and why I came from there.

Enough, I thought. It's consistent with everything I had discovered in my travels reported above. And if it was good enough me, I can only assume that it was good enough for Aldous, too.

And that, all of that, is what happened to me when I found myself a little crazy on too many scrips. *Scrip-crazy too* is another way of putting it.

"Take care with the mood-lifters," he whispered as the wheel-chair whisked him away.

Printed in Great Britain
by Amazon